ALPHAS' OMEGA

Creekside Township Rivals

Book 3

JT Fader

Published by Steambath Press
A Creekside Township Rivals Romance

Paperback published December 2023
ISBN-13: 978-1-998008-42-1

Chapter One | Bryant

I rolled over into a faceful of long grey and white fur. Grayson had decided to sleep in wolf form again. Why he was on the bed instead of down on the area carpet was anyone's guess.

I shoved him and he groaned.

"Grayson, seriously. Get off the bed. You're making a mess of the bedding."

When we first arrived two nights ago, I removed the layers of furs someone had been using on the bed. I preferred sheets and a comforter.

I did not appreciate Grayson's fur and muddy paws making laundry for me.

"Grayson!"

Grayson groaned again but this time climbed off the bed. He found a spot in front of the fireplace where a few embers were still burning, curled up, and went back to sleep.

I had the bed to myself.

We'd been sharing small spaces for 5 years now. In wolf form curled up together. Not in wolf form, sharing the same bed when we could get one for a night or two.

I stared up at the ceiling.

Now, I couldn't sleep.

I'd become used to him being near me at night. I almost wished he had shifted out of wolf form and stayed in bed with me. I felt alone without him.

Grayson and I met on the tundra when we were going after the same caribou. Food was scarce. We both knew the other was there. Instinctively, we had joined forces and taken it down together.

Feeding had led to a fight. We were both Alphas. We both held claim to the most tender parts of the kill. A few minutes of snarling, lunging, and biting had led to Grayson backing down.

I'd cleaned out and eaten every piece of the innards, leaving Grayson to feed on tougher parts. Our bellies full, we found a protected spot and slept. After spending three days and nights eating and sleeping, it was time to head out. We'd spent a moment looking at each other.

I trotted off into the forest. And Grayson followed.

And that's the way our lives carried on for the next 5 years.

I sat up in bed.

Dammit.

I rolled off the bed and shifted into wolf form. Grayson grumbled a little at the disturbance but sighed with satisfaction as I curled up against him. His fur was warm and familiar. It soothed me; helped me put aside the guilt I felt for what happened to Adam. Playing any part in Adam's kidnapping had been misguided and selfish. Having Adam finally forgive me meant the world to me. Having my family back was more than I had hoped would ever happen.

Lucas, Jonas, Carina, and I had hunted together last night for the first time in years. Afterward, I'd been given the honor of meeting all of Lucas and Adam's pups. I couldn't believe there were 8. I'd been gone far too long. It had been Grayson's idea to return to my home.

I had half expected Adam to challenge me. I would have let him win.

I snorted.

Chances are, he might have won anyway. Lucas' fated Omega was a force. Witnessing him being dragged through the forest by a chain on his way to a gutting by Derek was an image that would never leave me. My urge to protect him had been strong.

Unstoppable.

My inner wolf had been screaming, "Fated mate," since I first set eyes on Adam. It had cut me deep when he didn't feel the same way about me.

It wasn't unheard of; only one wolf feeling the pull of a fated mate. Our sire's brother had the same thing happen to him in his youth. He'd decided to leave Creekside when the wolf he yearned for as his fated mate was drawn to another. He'd never claimed a wolf after that.

I was lucky. For some reason, my pull toward Adam as my fated mate dissipated once I left Creekside. It took years to forget him, but I did. I hadn't felt it again, the pull toward a wolf.

I moved my muzzle closer to Grayson. I liked the smell of him. It reminded me of all the hunts we had been on together and the cold nights we had curled up against each other.

Our friendship was deep. On a wolf level. We rarely spent time out of wolf form. Talking hadn't been something we were interested in doing. Sometimes at night when we'd been offered an actual bed, Grayson would hum songs from his youth. The first couple of times, it annoyed me. After a few nights listening to him, I grew to long for it. It meant he was happy.

Being back in Creekside meant we'd spend a lot of time out of wolf form. We both felt obligated to help support my family and the pack. We needed to earn a living. Grayson felt a draw toward doing something in construction. Maybe painting. I'd agreed to set up a business with him.

I settled in.

Curled up against Grayson, sleep took me.

I WAS UP WITH THE SUN. Jonas had invited me to join them for breakfast at their house. I shifted, dressed, and headed out. Grayson had already left by the time I opened my eyes.

Likely, off to chase down some small game.

I set off through the trees. It was a gorgeous fall morning. The sun was bright, creating shadows and slivers of dancing light on the forest floor littered with leaves. The birds were happy and singing. My inner wolf nudged me, wanting me to shift and join them.

Not this morning. I needed to maintain my shifted form. I adjusted the collar of my coat. Clothes were irritating. Grayson and I had spent the last two months in them, though. I had needed a break from our life as wild wolves. Grayson had been supportive, as usual.

He hadn't asked me what the issue was. He'd abandoned wolf life and found himself a job. Not a moment of complaint. Our friendship might have been challenged by my decision. Instead, we'd never been closer. Spending time out of wolf form meant we could talk to each other.

Grayson had told me about his young wolfhood and how his pack had disbanded when their numbers were depleted due to a lack of pups. He was only 16 when he was told to find his own way in life. Being forced into a life as a lone wolf haunted him. Even his sire and his carrier had gone their separate ways. It was a complete destruction of their pack.

After hearing his story, I'd become more protective of Grayson. He'd been relying on himself for far too long. He needed a pack leader. I became that for him. The night that followed my declaration of leadership found him humming us both to sleep.

I crossed the clearing. Lucas' large log home was straight ahead. Next to it were two smaller log homes, one belonging to our sister Carina. At the far left, a new build, craftsman style. I laughed. Leave it to Jonas to do something different than everyone else.

The sound of a human baby crying met me as I approached the door. I pushed down my prejudice. If Jonas was happy with a human, I wasn't going to judge. Jonas had always been his own wolf. Living life on his own terms. Humans had always figured into that equation.

Now he was mated to one.

I knocked on the door. It was answered by a flustered Jonas, bouncing a bundle of screaming fury over one shoulder.

"Hey, Bryant. Welcome to this morning's fresh hell."

I followed Jonas inside. "Do they always do that? Human babies? Scream?"

"Only when they're hungry, angry, sad, lonely, or need their diaper changed."

"You can't let her out into the backyard to her business?"

Jonas glared at me. "She can't walk yet, Bryant."

Oh right.

"When *will* she walk?"

"Not for another year, at least."

My eyebrows jumped up. That was a long time to be carrying around a pup.

Baby.

Right. "You have to carry a baby until then?"

"No, she'll start crawling in a few months. Which will bring on its own set of challenges according to Damon. We'll have to *baby-proof* the place?"

"You're afraid she's going to chew on wires?"

Again with the glare.

"Here." Jonas handed the baby to me. "Don't drop her. I need to start the coffee."

The bundle felt strange in my arms. Furless arms and legs sticking out of clothes. I wasn't sure what to do with it. I tried bouncing it like I'd seen Jonas doing.

That seemed to calm it down a little bit.

"Why is it screaming? Which one of those things is bothering it?"

"Her. Jane."

"Right, sorry. Which one is causing all of *her* screaming?"

"Hungry. I'll feed her in a second. Coffee first."

Jonas buzzed around the kitchen, pouring water into a coffee pot, filling the basket with coffee grounds, and flicking on the machine. He reached for the baby.

"Here. I'll feed her. Damon will be down in a second."

Damon.

I had a question that had been rolling around in my mind.

"How did Damon do it … claim you?"

Jonas laughed. "You want the details of him mating with me?"

God, no.

"No. How did he bite you?"

"His wolf ancestry meant his incisors were a little longer than a regular human's. He broke the skin just fine … both times."

I grunted. "He claimed you twice?"

Jonas smiled at me. "That was just the first two times. I won't go into details, but our mating often leads to a voracious desire to taste each other's blood."

Yeah, okay. Too much information.

"I don't want to hear about it."

Jonas sat on the sofa, lifted his shirt on one side, lowered the flap on some kind of padded contraption he was wearing on his chest, and positioned the baby.

I wrinkled my nose as the wriggling little being started to suckle.

"I smell coffee." A voice called from the bottom of the stairs.

"It'll be ready in a few minutes," Jonas replied.

"I would have made it. Jane sounds like she's in fine form."

"Another morning of bliss," Jonas replied.

The human Damon entered the kitchen. He was tall but not broad. Whatever wolf ancestry he had, it hadn't emerged in his size. I could snap him like a twig.

He was perfectly sized for my brother, though.

And my Jonas loved him.

Set your damned bias aside.

"Good morning, Damon."

Damon extended his hand and I shook it.

"You sleeping all right in that cabin?" he asked.

"Had the fire banked for the night. By morning we were shifted back to our furs."

"Grayson, right?"

I nodded. "Yeah, he was off hunting by the time I woke. He's an early starter. Usually has a fresh rabbit for me when I wake up."

"You're good friends."

"Spent the last 5 years together, so yeah."

"It was nice you had someone," Jonas said. "I never liked the idea of you out there on your own." He lifted the baby onto his shoulder and patted her back until she burped.

"There you go, my sweet girl," Jonas cooed.

"When are you starting her on meat?" I asked.

Jeezus, that glare from Jonas again.

"I'll be chest-feeding her for at least a year. Maybe longer. In a few months, we'll start introducing her to pablum cereals. Then fruits, vegetables … and pureed *cooked* meats."

"Human food."

"Yeah." Jonas lifted the baby so I could see her face. "Does she look like a wolf to you?"

"Do you think she'll be able to shift?"

I turned to the stove area of the kitchen. Whatever Damon had started cooking smelled good. I'd detected the human food item before at Jonas' restaurant *Growlers*.

"Time will tell," Jonas replied. "I hope she doesn't go through the shift pattern in reverse. Shift to wolf form when she turns five and then stay that way until she's sixteen. That would mess up her schooling. She'd miss the whole teenage experience."

"I wish I could have missed my teenage experience," Damon said. He used tongs to flip what he was cooking. Then he moved to the fridge and removed a plastic container.

He popped the lid. Inside were some beautiful raw venison ribs.

"I'm with you on that," I replied. "I was so happy to shift early at fifteen."

"You used to torment me," Jonas said. He reclined the baby in his arms and latched her onto the other side of his chest. She was certainly a good feeder. "Shifting and cornering me."

"You were easy to tease. You were so small."

Jonas stuck out his tongue. "Compact."

"Our bodies fit perfectly together," Damon said.

I waved my hand. "Don't want to know."

Damon chuckled and lifted strips of sizzling meat from the hot pan he'd been using. He dabbed them with a paper towel, then walked across the kitchen with one piece.

I gasped as he fed the cooked meat to Jonas.

My brother was being influenced by all the humans in his home. Next, I'd catch him eating vegetables. That would throw his body right off. He wouldn't be that reckless.

"Do you want to try a piece?" Damon asked me.

I furrowed my brow and shook my head. "I'm a purest. Meat, eggs, and berries."

"What about Grayson?"

"Same."

"I was hoping he would join us this morning," Jonas said. "I'd like to meet him."

"He's shy. Just give him a bit of time." I wouldn't force Grayson to interact with my family. He'd come around at his own speed. I'd never ask him to do anything that would make him feel uncomfortable. As his impromptu pack leader, his happiness was my responsibility.

"Whenever he's ready," Jonas replied. The baby was back over his shoulder. I shivered in disgust as thick cream exited the baby and coated Jonas' shirt.

I turned back to the counter.

Damon smiled at me. "I take it pups don't spit up."

"Not unless they're sick."

"Jane drank too much milk. She's very much a wolf in that regard." He pushed the plastic container with the ribs toward me. "Help yourself."

I inhaled and my wolf saw red. When I looked down next, the container only held meatless bones. I'd been hungrier than I'd thought I'd be after hunting with my siblings last night.

Jonas wandered into the kitchen without the baby. I looked toward the sofa. On the floor in front of it, in a colorful chair, Jonas had set the baby. She was nodding off as the chair bounced.

I shook my head.

Human babies were strange.

Jonas pulled up a stool beside me at the counter and bit into a bloody bison steak Damon had set out. I growled, claiming feeding rights. He growled back and moved away from me.

"No fights in my kitchen," Damon said.

I pulled my gaze from the steak. Damon slid a cardboard container of quail's eggs toward me. It was enough to distract me. I hadn't had a feed of eggs since spring.

I dug in.

I would have felt bad finishing them all. Grayson loved quail's eggs. I left four.

"Do you mind if I take these to Grayson?"

"They're all yours," Damon replied. "We keep stocked up on them. They're Adam's favorite. They remind him of home."

There was still a slight pull there. "Adam really is happy?"

"Those two," Jonas said, his lips covered in blood. "They're nauseating they're so in love."

"Hence the 8 pups," Damon added.

"That settles my guilt a little."

"We're not going to talk about that anymore," Jonas replied. "The past is the past. You're back. And you seem content. Perhaps your Omega is out there still."

That seemed unlikely. And I wasn't sure I needed a disruption like that in my life. Jonas was right. I was content. I liked the friendship Grayson and I had grown together.

Even if I never found my Omega, at least I had Grayson at my side.

Chapter Two | Grayson

I slept better after Bryant decided to join me on the floor. After Bryant made up with his family, he'd gone on a hunt with them—leaving me behind to wander back to the cabin on my own. It had felt strange to be away from him. I had spent 5 years at his side.

Loyal.

Now that we were in Creekside, I wouldn't have him to myself anymore.

Bryant had flicked his muzzle against my hip again and woke me. It stirred something in me. Out of wolf form, his face's proximity to my cock would be problematic. It's why I preferred to sleep in wolf form with him. The temptation to touch him with bare hands was too extreme.

I didn't blame him for kicking me out of bed. It was fall and my winter coat was starting to grow in early. There was a lot of fur. I tended to shed. Bryant hated strands of it on his blankets.

I would do anything Bryant asked of me. When we first met, he had intrigued me. He was the most tortured wolf I'd ever come across. After three days of feeding, I'd decided to follow him.

My confused heart had led the way.

Whining and prodding at him each night, it had taken weeks for Bryant to finally shift and tell me about his pain;

about Adam. How he'd almost had his unrequited fated mate killed.

He hadn't spoken about it again. We rarely spoke about anything, spending most of our time in wolf form. There was no telepathic link between us. The few conversations we'd had over the years, I could count on two hands. Until two months ago when we'd taken a break from the forest at his insistence, found some odd jobs, and rented a room in a boarding house

We'd received an odd look from the boarding house owner when we told him we wanted to share a room. We explained it away, citing the lack of money for two rooms.

The owner didn't look convinced. We were obviously two Alphas and Alpha males didn't form mated pairs. Everyone knew that. Maybe I'd looked too longingly at Bryant as he spoke to him.

The past two months of living and working together out of wolf form where we were more inclined to talk and tease each other a little cemented my feelings for Bryant.

I was in love with an Alpha male.

I was in love with Bryant.

Chapter Three | Hunter

Riverton Township could be a real drag. I had to be creative to keep myself occupied. Being in my early 20s, my friends were quick to tease me. But when I wasn't working, I liked to knit.

I'd grown up in Riverton. Creekside's sleepy cousin township. Entertainment had to be self-propelled. If you didn't make your own fun, you'd soon die of boredom.

I leaned back in my chair and finished the last few knots. Another scarf. I had made enough of them to supply an army. I had a different colored one for every one of my many outfits.

Scarves and cute little beanies.

I was set for winter once again. Not that anyone noticed other than to whisper behind their hands to their companions about me and my effeminate mannerisms.

I stood out.

And I didn't care.

I was a wolf. I had the advantage if any humans decided to mess with me. I'd had to defend myself a few times with human bullies yelling their word *faggot* at me as they came after me.

My sexual preference for males had no equivalent of the human slur in the wolf world. The only relationship that was frowned upon in *my* world was the mating of two Alpha males.

I'd been up early to finish the scarf. I was headed to Creekside today to paint the living room of a human I'd worked for before. It was an hour's drive away but most of my jobs came from Creekside. Riverton had very few homes or businesses that required my trade.

I'd often thought of moving townships.

But all of my friends were in Riverton. Wolves I'd known my entire life. The thought of starting fresh somewhere new didn't appeal to me. The only consideration for making a move was the chance of meeting my Alpha. He wasn't in Riverton, that's for sure.

The thought of finding an Alpha with a shared interest in each other excited *and* terrified me. Not sure what I'd do with him. Supposedly, it came naturally—mating.

I had no idea.

I'd only ever mated with my hand.

Chapter Four | Bryant

I headed to Lucas' from Jonas' place. If Grayson and I were going to start a business, we needed a few things. Things neither of us could afford. Hence, I was visiting my pack leader.

I felt bad asking. Lucas and Adam had 8 pups to take care of. I knew they were probably strapped for cash. I also knew Lucas took his position as pack leader seriously. The protocol was for wolves in the pack to come to the pack leader if they needed help financially.

If he couldn't help me, someone else in the pack might be able to.

I knocked on the door. Instead of a baby crying, the other side of *this* door was overrun by barking pups. It was like having an extra noisy doorbell—pups.

Adam pulled open the door. I wasn't sure if he was upset to see me or not. He waved me in and headed off through the front entry, calling Lucas' name.

Maybe he was just busy.

I broke out in a sweat, heat drifting out of the top of my shirt and dampening my back. What if he hadn't forgiven me? What if he hated me? What if he convinced Lucas to throw me out?

"Bryant!"

I snapped out of my thoughts. Lucas was standing in front of me. He had his hands on his hips, frowning. I hadn't heard him come into the front entry and say my name.

"Sorry, Alpha. Lost in my thoughts."

"Did you have a nice breakfast at Jonas and Damon's?"

"The baby is loud."

Lucas laughed. "Yes, Jane has a set of lungs on her."

"Do you think she'll be able to shift someday?"

"I almost hope she won't be able to. Life is much easier as a human."

"A human with a wolf carrier?"

"Papa."

"Who?"

"Jonas is Jane's Papa."

I rolled my eyes. "Of course, he is." My brother had fully immersed himself in human life. The human mate, the human baby, the human style of home. Being called Papa.

"Come in," Lucas said and led me to the living room. "Can I get you a coffee?"

"No, I'm off coffee." I found a spot on the sofa. "Spent too many years without it."

"You stayed in wolf form for most of your time away?"

"Almost all of it until 2 months ago."

Lucas lowered himself into an armchair and leaned forward. "What was that like?"

I smiled. "Liberating. All of your worries melt away."

"Sounds restorative."

"It was." I looked down at my hands. "Still thought about Adam, though."

"You longed for him?"

"Painfully. It wasn't until I told Grayson about what happened … about what I'd done. What almost happened to Adam—that I started releasing thoughts of him."

"Grayson helped you through that?"

I shrugged. "Not by talking or anything. I just knew he was there for me. He hadn't judged me for my selfishness and my blind desire to possess Adam—my brother's fated mate."

"But you're sure you're past that now?"

I looked up and caught Lucas' gaze. "My only interest in Adam now is to admire how happy he makes you. How you've built a life and a home together. And a family filled with pups."

"Yeah, we've got that pup-filled family bit down."

"I can't believe you have 8."

Just as I spoke those words—three of them raced through the room, chasing a ball. I had to tuck my feet in to avoid being run over. They tumbled over each other, one of them grabbed the ball—and they were off back to the kitchen.

I jumped as something crashed onto the floor in there and Adam barked out an order to *slow down*. My brother was living in absolute chaos. He didn't seem the slightest bit bothered.

"Is this a social visit?" Lucas asked.

I refocused my attention on him. "No, I'm coming to you as my pack leader."

"What do you need?"

"Grayson and I want to start a painting business. There isn't one in town."

"What would you need?"

I had a list in my head. "A van, scaffolding, and tarps, brushes, rollers, etcetera."

"How much money do you need?"

Grayson had checked the newspaper. There was a van for sale that would suit us. It was 15 years old but the seller stated it was mechanically sound. New muffler, carburetor, and tires.

"$12,000 would get us started."

Lucas sighed. "That sounds about right." He rose from his chair. "I trust you to be conservative with your start-up costs. You know how trade businesses run."

"I'll save the scaffolding until we need it."

"And the van?"

"Found one already."

"How long have you been back?"

"Two days. I wanted a day before I approached you."

"I didn't catch your scent."

"I sent Grayson into town for a newspaper and to make the phone call."

"Sent him? Has he been *your* pack?"

"He bows to me, yes."

"I'm anxious to meet him."

"Like I told Jonas … Grayson is shy. I won't push him."

"You care about him."

"We've been through a lot over the past 5 years."

I could tell where the furrow of Lucas' brow was going. We'd seen a lot of that in the human world. We were obviously two Alphas. And we were close … but just friends.

"Anything going on there?" Lucas asked after a few moments of scrutinizing me.

"No, I assure you, Grayson is not my type. Plus, he's an Alpha male."

"You let Derek, an Alpha male, claim *and* mate with you."

I crossed my arms. I wasn't interested in Grayson that way. Once I was settled, I'd be heading into town looking for Omegas to rut with. "Under duress, Lucas. Grayson is *just* a friend."

"I wouldn't judge. I learned my lesson with Jonas. He and Damon are perfect for each other."

"I can assure you, that is *not* the case."

"Okay. I just need to know what's happening in my pack."
Redirect.

"So, the $12,000. Are you able to invest in our business?"

Lucas nodded. "Yeah, that's no problem. Our coffers are still pretty full after all that new construction work years back. Plus, you're my brother. I'd find it to give to you."

I reached out my hand and shook Lucas'. "I appreciate that."

"Head down to the office with me. I have the money in the safe."

"Still don't like banks?"

"I don't trust humans to protect my money. Too easy for it to disappear."

Fair enough. All it would take is an uprising against us and any assets we had that were controlled by humans might be taken from us. It's why we always owned our business buildings and homes outright. Even if everyone in the pack had to contribute to purchase a property.

Collective purchasing power was an incredible benefit of pack life.

I held back as Lucas opened the safe. Inside were neat stacks of paper money, divided into bundles by white paper bands. Lucas grabbed twelve of them. The removal barely made a dent.

It made me proud.

My brother was a fearsome and responsible leader.

Lucas pulled a white plastic grocery bag out from under his desk. He carefully set the money inside it and handed it to me. "Remember," he said. "Be conservative."

"My middle name will be frugal, I promise."

He patted my shoulder and led me to the front door. He surprised me by hugging me.

"I'm so glad you're back, brother," he whispered in my ear.

"I won't let you down. I promise."

"Okay." Lucas stepped away. "Go start that business."

One last thing.

"My truck?"

"It's in the shed. I've been starting it every week since you left. Tires might need attention."

Lucas had been expecting me to come home. He knew I wouldn't be able to stay away forever. He had been hopeful of my return. My brother loved me.

I pulled him back into my arms. "Thank you, Alpha."

He pounded my shoulders. "Enough. I have to get back to wrangling pups."

I took a deep breath, inhaling the scent of family. As I walked to the shed to retrieve my truck, I felt a new optimism. I couldn't wait to tell Grayson that we could start our business. He'd be quietly pleased on the outside, but his eyes … his eyes always gave away what he was feeling.

His eyes had been telling a new story of late.

I circled my truck and took a look at the tires. Lucas had been keeping them inflated. The truck should be fine to drive. I leaned against the driver's door and thought about Grayson and what Lucas had asked me. Grayson's gaze, when he looked at me, *had* changed recently.

I wasn't sure I wanted to know why.

I hadn't detected any change in Grayson's scent. Although, even fully aroused, Grayson's scent was light. Barely perceptible. I could have easily missed a change in his attitude toward me.

I pushed those thoughts aside. We were about to embark on a new business. Grayson knew how to paint, so he'd be teaching me. The log homes our pack always built didn't have sheetrock on the walls. There had been no opportunity for me to learn any painting skills.

I jogged through the trees back to the cabin.

Grayson was shifted out of wolf form and naked, standing near the bed. I looked away. He was partially aroused. Typically I didn't see him like that out of wolf form. And not after the question Lucas had asked me. I peered back at him. My gaze wandered down his spine.

"Put it away." I pushed my way into the cabin past a wooden door that needed to be replaced. It often stuck on the flagstone doorway. It would be a repair for later.

Grayson was quick to dress. "Caught the scent of an Omega. Distracted me."

"I'd rather not discuss it."

"Any luck?"

Thank God.

We had switched topics to things I'd rather be talking about.

"Lucas invested in our business. Enough to get us started."

There it was. My gaze focused on Grayson's face. That shy lift of his lip on one side and the way his soft grey eyes crinkled when he was happy. It made me smile.

"When can we get the van?" he asked.

"Lucas took care of my truck while I was away. We can get the van any time."

"I told him we might be there today." Grayson dug around in his shirt pocket. "I have his address." He held out a piece of paper to me. "It's in someplace called Riverton."

"That's the next township over. Take us about an hour."

"Can we go now?"

I took the paper and glanced at it. The address would be easy to find. There were very few streets in Riverton. Drive around a little and we'd find it.

"Let's go." I held the door open for Grayson to leave the cabin. It was my station to go out the door first but I liked to throw him off on occasion. It made him blush.

It felt good to start up my truck. It rumbled to life as if I hadn't been away from it for over 6 years. She was a bit dusty, but I could give her a good wash when we returned.

Grayson made a nervous grab for the dashboard as I gunned the truck down the driveway. He'd been running as a wolf for most of 25 years. Trucks might as well be foreign to him.

There had been three times in his life when he had lived out of wolf form. Once in his 20s when he'd picked up his painting skills. Once in his 30s when he'd needed a stretch of rutting. And the third time, when I'd insisted I needed time away from running around in my furs.

Being away from his wolf form was uncomfortable for Grayson. But he knew it was important to me. Thankfully, as the sole member of my pack, he had agreed to continue following me.

I glanced over at him gripping the door handle and staring out through the windscreen. He caught me looking and his expression changed from discomfort to fear.

"Watch the road!" he yelled.

"I can watch the road and check on you at the same time. Are you all right?"

"I'm nervous, that's all. Haven't been in a truck in a while."

"Try to relax. I'm a good driver."

"When you're watching the road maybe."

"I promise not to look at you."

Grayson crossed his arms. "Good."

I grinned. After saying that, now I wanted to look. To see his profile. A profile I knew so well. A profile that had been on the pillow next to mine so many times.

A profile that brought me peace.

I cleared my throat and concentrated on the road. After a very quiet hour, Riverton came into view. I drove down the main street. I knew there were a few streets behind the main drag. I made a right turn. Two blocks down, I found the street we were looking for.

345 Richter.

It was an old dumpy house painted in the full array of rainbow colors. Every color of the human queer community flag. I groaned as a figure left the house and stepped onto the driveway.

The guy was the size of a human male and muscular. Like a spunky athletic mouse.

I inhaled.

Wolf—Omega.

Then why with all the damned rainbow colors? Was he deliberately trying to piss off his human neighbors? His pack leader hadn't been keeping tabs on him very well.

I climbed out of the truck. On the driveway was the van we were interested in purchasing. It looked in decent shape. As long as it ran, I wasn't too concerned about what it looked like.

The Omega approached. I looked him over. His facial features were pleasing—sensual. Dark blond hair, blue eyes, and plump lips. Those lips had probably seen a lot of action.

There was a sexuality pouring off him that was palpable.

He held out his hand. "Hunter."

"Bryant."

I shook his offered hand, making sure to remind him I was an Alpha. Standing there alone, I looked over my shoulder. Grayson was leaning against the truck. He was staring at Hunter.

"Grayson," I called to him.

He blinked and looked at me. "Alpha."

"Let's look at the van."

"Right." He pushed away from the truck but didn't approach. "Let's do that."

"Can you open her up for us?" I asked Hunter.

"Sure." Hunter unlocked the back doors and swung them open. Inside, the van was already set up for what we needed it for.

"What did you do with the van?"

"I have a painting business."

"Oh ... perfect. That's what we'll be using it for. Why are you selling?"

"Landed a big contract for the exterior of a church. It'll pay for a newer van for me."

"Wow. Lucky." I hoisted myself up and entered the van. "I didn't know Riverton had a church." Everything looked perfect. The sides were covered in plywood. Plenty of hooks and metal shelving for everything we'd need to bring with us to a job.

"Not in Riverton," Hunter replied. "The contract is in Creekside."

What?

I turned and growled at him. To his credit, he didn't even step back.

"Did you clear that with Lucas?"

"Didn't need to. There's no painting company in Creekside."

"There is now," Grayson said. I was glad he had finally decided to participate in the conversation. Even for Grayson, he'd been quiet.

"You're from Creekside?" Hunter asked.

"My brother is the leader of the East Creekside pack."

Hunter crossed his arms. "When did you start your business?"

The spunky mouse had guts. He wasn't afraid to confront an Alpha. All I needed to do was demand he obey. The words tickled the end of my tongue.

But he had piqued my curiosity.

"Today," I answered.

"My contract was signed last week."

I shifted from foot to foot and then leaped from the van. I approached Hunter. "So, you're telling me you're not going to back down and hand over the contract to us?"

Hunter crossed his arms. "Why on earth would I do that?"

"I'm an Alpha."

"You're not *my* Alpha."

"Who *is* your Alpha?"

Hunter bit down hard on his bottom lip. The fury in his eyes bored into me.

"I don't need one," he spat at me at last.

"That's debatable."

The mouse's fists balled up at his sides. "Do you want to buy the van or not?"

"$6000."

"$7500."

Obnoxious Omega playing hardball with me. "$6850."

"Fine. Deal."

We were both vibrating as we shook hands. I wasn't gentle with him. He gritted his teeth and accepted the grip of my hand.

Grayson.

What the hell was he doing? He hadn't moved from the side of the truck even though he had agreed to look at the van. Something had frozen him in place.

"Grayson, can you climb in the truck … count out the money for me." I turned back to Hunter. "Do you have change for $7000?"

He goddamned rolled his eyes at me.

"I can find $150." He turned toward the house. "Back in a second." His tight body entered his house. My truck door slammed. With the money in hand, Grayson gripped my shoulder.

"I'll drive the van," he said.

"You going to be all right doing that? Lucas and I can come back here tomorrow."

"I'll manage. It's a straight shot. No traffic. I'll be fine."

I had to know. "What the hell happened to you? You didn't leave the side of the truck. I would have appreciated you backing me up."

Grayson sighed. "His scent caught me off guard."

"Fated mate?"

Grayson shook his head. "No. It's nothing. I'm just in need of a good rut."

Hunter returned with the $150 in change. Grayson handed him the stacks of bills and our business was concluded. Mighty mouse handed the keys to me. I gave them to Grayson.

I put my hand on Grayson's shoulder.

"Don't crash the van," I warned him.

"We done?" Hunter asked.

I couldn't help myself. "Obey. Omega." Yeah, I could be an asshole sometimes, but this Omega needed to be put in his place.

Hunter crossed his arms. "Piss off."

I laughed. Fiesty. I liked that.

Hunter intrigued me.

"You're really going to keep that church contract?" I asked him.

"I secured the contract before you started your business. I don't owe you anything. I don't even know you. You say you're the East Creekside's leader's brother but you could be lying."

"Easy thing to check. Ask your leader, Mark."

Hunter shook his head. "We don't speak."

"You don't speak to your pack leader?"

"I'm his annoying cousin. We have our issues."

I grunted. That would explain the house's paint colors. This Omega had been left to do whatever he wanted. I wasn't sure whether to be annoyed or impressed.

"Why paint your house like that?" I asked him.

"The humans like to call me a *faggot*. I own it."

Yeah, okay … impressed.

"You can keep your contract but stay out of Creekside after that."

"Ha." Hunter placed his hands on his hips. "You afraid of a little competition?"

Now, I switched to annoyed.

"You know what? I'm not going to report you to my brother." I walked toward him. He held his ground. "Bring it on. We'll see who gets all the jobs."

"You don't have a chance. I'm going to crush you."

Hunter smiled at me. The shape of his mouth unsettled me. Partially descended canines pressed to his full lips. The urge to storm toward him and kiss those lips was strong.

Kiss him just to shut him up.

"Game is on." I waved at Grayson. He followed my direction and climbed into the driver's side of the van. It started on the first try. Now that we were competitors, I was surprised

Hunter didn't insist on canceling the sale of the van. He hadn't handed me the ownership paperwork yet.

He pulled it out of his back pocket and waved it in front of me.

"If I didn't want that newer van so bad," he said, "this wouldn't be happening."

I snatched the paperwork out of the air. "I would have found another vehicle."

"That's what I figure. I might as well benefit."

I spun and headed for my truck. "Enjoy the rest of your day." I hauled open my truck door.

"I will. I'll be preparing for that church job."

I growled and threw myself into my seat behind the wheel. Cheeky little bastard. As I pulled out of the driveway, I had a full-on private snarling session. My inner wolf had his hackles up.

I wasn't sure if it was anger or arousal that was coursing through me. Both emotions made my cock hard. Hunter had burrowed in under my skin.

Goddammit.

I wanted to rut him into the ground.

Chapter Five | Grayson

The drive back from Riverton was a bit harrowing. I hadn't driven a vehicle in over 15 years. Thankfully, there were few other cars on the road. I just needed to keep the van between the lines and maintain an acceptable speed. Bryant was driving behind me.

Parked in front of Lucas' house, I was able to relax and let my mind wander. The wolf we had bought the van from had stirred an emotion in me I'd never felt before.

I had felt an overwhelming need to protect him.

Hunter.

Bryant becoming annoyed with the young Omega had tested my loyalty toward him. Had tested my love for him. If their aggressive banter had led to a fight, I might have been inclined to take Hunter's side. I shook my head. No. My allegiance was to Bryant.

My driver's side door popped open.

"You all right?" Bryant set his hand on my arm. Tendrils of warm tingles traveled to my shoulder and across my chest. My inner wolf groaned.

My love for him was complete and unshakeable.

"I'll recover. You drive from now on, though."

"I think that's best. You were driving the speed of a decrepit aging wolf."

Bryant stepped back and I climbed out of the van. "I got the van here in one piece. That's the important thing." Bryant looked distracted. "What's next?"

"Um …." Bryant blinked at me. "We'll use Lucas' computer and print up some flyers."

"Right now?" That would mean going into the house.

"Better sooner than later. You don't have to come with me."

I nodded. "No, I will. I suppose I should meet Lucas."

"Only if you're ready."

I looked toward the house. A rather robust wolf was looking out through the window at us. I couldn't put it off any longer. At the very least, I needed to thank him for investing in our business.

"I'm ready."

Bryant smiled at me. I loved when he did that. It was a heartfelt smile. He only dolled them out when he was truly pleased by something or someone. The wolf equivalent would be him nudging my muzzle with his. I preferred that—when he touched me.

I followed Bryant up the steps to the door. One knock and the interior of the house erupted in sound. Bryant had told me there were 8 pups. Lucas' Omega was excessively fertile.

And the Omega had been Bryant's fated mate. I was more nervous about meeting Adam than I was about meeting his mate and pack leader, Lucas. Bryant told me he felt no connection to Adam anymore but the theory hadn't been tested until last night at the family meeting.

He reported back that he had felt nothing.

A beautiful muscular Omega opened the door. A furry band of pups danced at his feet. Yipping and leaping up, trying to get his attention. He didn't break his stride as he led us into the house.

"Don't mind the younger ones," Adam said. "They have more energy than sense at this point."

"You have two who have shifted?" I asked.

"Yes, Maddox and Briana. They're around here somewhere." Adam looked me up and down. He extended his hand. "I'm Adam."

"Grayson." I shook his hand. His hand was almost larger than mine. He *was* a big Omega. Bryant had said he was a force. Now I knew what he meant. He exuded confidence.

Kind of like Hunter.

I sighed. I'd probably never be in the young wolf's presence again. Bryant would make sure of that. Avoid speaking to Hunter if we happened to encounter him.

Rightly so. Hunter had threatened to scoop all the jobs in Creekside. Realistically, both sides knew that wasn't possible. Customers would pick and choose based on their own set of criteria. Hunter likely had more experience than us but I was exemplary in my skill. Word would get around. We'd make enough money to help support Lucas' pack.

"Grayson," a powerful voice boomed.

I focused on the imposing figure entering the room. He was a magnificent Alpha. Whereas Bryant was dark-featured and gorgeous broody, Lucas, with the looks of an Adonis, had dark hair and eyes, but there was light behind them. He was fulfilled and satisfied with his life.

I longed for that light in Bryant's eyes.

I nearly stuttered as I took his hand. "Yes. Grayson."

"I've been looking forward to meeting you," Lucas said.

"Sorry, it took me a day. Needed to get my head on straight. Arriving at a new location with the intention of settling is new for me."

"You *do* plan to stay?"

"It's time I set down roots. I'm almost 50."

"You've been living as a wolf for a long time."

"Too long."

"What are your long-term plans?"

I felt like shrugging but Lucas would be expecting an answer. There was what I *wanted* and what was feasible and realistic. I wanted a life with Bryant. In my heart and my bed. That wasn't going to happen. Bryant had never shown any interest in me. In wolf form, he often curled up against me but that was just his wolf encouraging him to do so. It was a comfort thing.

Out of wolf form, sharing a human bed, Bryant kept to himself. Sometimes we woke with our arms and legs entwined but he was quick to move away from me.

He'd never be more than a friend.

"I noticed a boarding house in town," I answered. "I might get a room there. Find myself an Omega. Join a pack house and settle down. Start a family of pups."

Lucas nodded. That answer appeared to please him.

That voice inside screamed at me. Following that plan would leave me dead inside. My heart belonged to Bryant. I'd find more peace if I lived the rest of my life alone.

I decided the boarding house part of my story was a good idea. I couldn't bear to live with Bryant anymore. It hurt too much. Living out of wolf form meant my emotions would be more acute. I couldn't immerse myself in wolf survival mode except at night. Nights I would rather spend in Bryant's arms. Have Bryant kissing and mating with me all night long.

My cock throbbed.

"You're excited about the new business?" Lucas asked me.

"Yes, and thank you. I appreciate your generosity in getting us started."

I watched Lucas' features. He hadn't detected my arousal. Few did. That's why I didn't temper it. Even around Bryant. Lying naked in bed with him more often than not made me hard.

He hadn't noticed other than leaping away from my morning wood.

"You've painted before," Lucas said.

"For five years, back while in my 20s. I'm confident I still have the skill."

"You'll be teaching Bryant."

I smiled. "Sure … if he's teachable."

Lucas laughed. "His ability to learn is adequate."

"Hey." Bryant shoved me playfully. "I'll be fine." He kept his hand on my back. "Just start me with the easy stuff. No edging." He moved his hand away and I could breathe again.

"It was a pleasure meeting you, Grayson."

"You as well."

We were being dismissed.

"One last thing," Bryant said. "We need to make some flyers. Can we use your computer and printer? If you can spare the paper, I'd like to print at least fifty."

"Sure. There's even colored paper in the office." Lucas stepped aside. "Go ahead. The sooner you get those flyers out, the sooner you'll start making some money."

"Thank you, Alpha," Bryant replied then headed down a hallway. I followed after nodding my thanks to Lucas. It felt good to be part of a pack. I hadn't expected that.

Bryant pulled a chair up in front of the computer screen. He put his hand on the mouse and started clicking on things. Images popped up. I was utterly confused. I'd never used a computer.

"What are we going to call our business?" Bryant asked me.

"Keep it simple. Creekside Painting. Potential customers will know we're local."

"Good idea." He typed it on the top of a document and changed the way it looked, making the words bigger and more like a real advert. "We're going to have to use Lucas' phone number. There's no way to get a phone into the cabin. He won't mind if we use his answering machine."

"If I move out to the boarding house, maybe we could get a phone strung into my room."

Bryant turned his chair to face me. "You would actually do that? Move out? I thought when you outlined that plan you were trying to appease my brother."

"I was … but I think I should move out of the cabin. If we're planning on settling here, we'll both be looking for an Omega. At the very least we'll want to bring rutting partners home."

Bryant furrowed his brow at me. "Maybe this was a bad idea … coming home."

"Why? You needed to clear things up with Adam. It'll take a while still until he's completely comfortable with you. That was the plan. We agreed on the plan."

"I didn't know that meant we were going to go our separate ways."

"We're not. We have a business together. We'll see each other every day."

"And at night?"

It was my turn to furrow my brow. What about at night? We could avoid the awkward sleeping conditions if I moved into my own space. I wouldn't lie awake longing to touch him.

"I wouldn't have to listen to your snoring," I replied. "That's what."

"I'd miss you."

Jeezus.

I hated mixed signals like that. Sometimes Bryant dropped little spatterings of them. I knew they meant nothing. It was just a bad habit of his.

"You'll survive."

"So … you're really going to do it. Leave me alone."

"It's what's best for both of us."

Bryant sighed. "When?"

"I'll drop in while we're handing out flyers and see if there's a room available."

Bryant nodded and turned back to the computer. His movements, clicking and typing, were slow after that conversation. I hadn't expected my decision to hit him so hard.

Fifty flyers in hand, we headed back out in the truck and drove into town. We decided to start walking at one end of Main Street and cover both sides. We'd hit the other residential areas from the truck. There were quite a few houses scattered throughout the treed areas.

My side of the street included the boarding house. I could do two things at once. Hand the flyer to the boarding house manager and find out about a room. After we finished the main street, we would need to stop to feed. It would be approaching early evening when we were done.

I walked through the boarding house door. It was a comfortable space. A kindly-looking Beta wolf approached. She was aged. I felt immediately comfortable with her.

"Can I help you?" she asked.

"Yes. I just moved into town."

She smiled at me. "Welcome."

"Thank you."

"And you're looking for a room?"

"Yes. Do you have one?"

"You're lucky. I had someone move out yesterday."

My stomach fluttered. I was really doing this. After 5 years at Bryant's side, I was gathering the courage to protect my heart. Spending days with him was the most I could handle.

"I'd like to look at it, please."

"Wonderful." She waved her hand. "Follow me."

Up the wooden stairs, we climbed. To each side, loud flowery wallpaper that might have been there for a hundred years. The room she showed me was quaint. It had everything I needed. I had no belongings other than the few sets of clothes Bryant said I could take from the cabin.

"I'll take it."

"I'll need $100 upfront. $400 a month after that. Two meals included. Breakfast and dinner. I'll accommodate your diet but you'll want to supplement it at *Growlers*."

"Jonas' restaurant?"

"That's the one." She locked the suite after we exited it. "You're Bryant's friend, right?"

I had forgotten how quickly word circulated in a wolf pack. This Beta wolf knew everything I had told Lucas. It felt strange to lose my anonymity.

"Yes, I'm Grayson."

Again that warm smile. "You can call me Mama, Alpha."

"Thank you, Mama. I'll have the money for you in a couple of hours. I can do the full amount right away. Is it all right if I move in right away? My current sleeping arrangement isn't ideal."

"Sharing a small cabin with Bryant ... I can imagine."

I held in my emotions. We'd only spent two nights in that cabin. But we'd spent two months in similar accommodations. My heart was breaking at the thought of leaving him behind.

"Yeah, it's been challenging."

"Bring me the money and you can sleep here tonight."

"Perfect." I pasted on a smile. "Thank you." I looked down at the stack of papers in my hands. "Oh." I lifted one to hand her. "Bryant and I have started a painting company."

Mama took the paper. "I'll keep this in mind. Some of the rooms need to be freshened."

"Let me know if you decide to do that." I pointed at the door. "I need to get back out there. I've got my side of the street to finish yet. Bryant will be waiting for me."

"Hopefully we'll see you tonight."

"I'll be here." I stepped outside. Bryant wouldn't withhold the deposit and first month's rent from me. He might be upset about me moving out but he also wanted me to be happy.

He'd been a good pack leader that way. My happiness was paramount in everything we did. He valued my input. Even when he wanted to leave our furs behind for a while, he'd asked me first. I knew if I'd said *no*, we would have continued our lives in wolf form.

I finished my side of the street, tucking flyers into mailboxes of houses, and walking in and introducing myself to businesses. By the time I finished, Bryant was pacing at the end of the street.

"You finished?" he asked.

"All done."

"And you went to see Mama?"

"I have a room starting tonight. Just need $500 for the deposit and rent."

Bryant grunted. "We can take that from the money we have."

"Thank you."

"It's as much your money as mine. No need to thank me."

"Then let's buy some food."

Bryant zoned out in communication with someone for a second.

"Jonas is working tonight," he said. "You can meet him."

I exhaled. "Okay." Today was a day of introductions. Jonas was mated with a human. I wasn't sure what to expect from him. Would he act more human than wolf?

"*Growlers* is just down here." Bryant led the way. Jonas' restaurant looked like a classic diner. Big windows. Booths with red pleather seats along the outside. Black and white checkered floor. Metal-rimmed tables with Formica red surfaces and metal chairs with black padded seats.

The restaurant was half full.

Bryant strolled up to the counter. Racing around behind it, a delicate almost pretty Omega with raven black hair and the dark gentle eyes of a deer. His lashes were stunning.

Bryant leaned against the counter. "Hey, Jonas."

"Give me a sec, Bryant," Jonas said and piled four plates of food onto his arms. I was impressed by his ability to get everything safely to a table on the far side of the room.

He flew back behind the counter and wiped some brown liquid off one arm.

Jonas lit up as his gaze caught my presence.

"And you must be Grayson," he said.

I couldn't help but smile. Jonas' enthusiastic attitude was contagious.

"That I am."

"Have you been keeping my brother out of trouble all these years?"

"Impossible."

"True." Jonas turned to Bryant. "I hope you weren't too miserable to live with."

"I was a joy," Bryant answered.

"Doubtful. Are you here to eat?"

"Starving," Bryant answered.

"You're in luck. I have some bison rump roasts I haven't cooked yet."

My stomach grumbled. "I think I like your brother, Bryant."

"Ah, he's tolerable. We'll have two of those roasts."

"You'll have to share the booth," Jonas said. "Plenty of room left."

"Won't be the first time." Bryant waved me along to the back of the restaurant to a booth hidden out of sight of the main room. He came to an abrupt stop, reached back, and put his hand on my chest. In the booth, a mid-20s wolf was seeing red and tearing through a bloody steak.

Hunter.

My heart pattered around in my chest. It was the closest I had ever been to him. I'd held back deliberately at the truck. His scent was incredible. Then and now.

My cock thickened.

I inhaled deeper and stepped back—confused.

Bryant's scent.

He was aroused too.

We were probably a sight. Standing there, dumbfounded, staring at the young wolf. Neither of us could pull out of it, though. It was too pleasurable to watch him feed.

Finally, Bryant made a move and slid onto the seat opposite Hunter. I waited for direction from him. Bryant indicated I needed to sit beside Hunter, boxing him in.

My body quivered as I sat near the source of the scent that was driving me crazy.

Hunter's inner wolf sensed me. He growled and slid away from me, the steak gripped tightly in his hands. We had no intention of taking his meat. His carnality was adorable.

We waited while Hunter finished. Jonas must have sensed our state of arousal because he stayed away. We could feed later.

Things were about to get interesting.

Chapter Six | Hunter

When I returned to my surroundings, I was surprised to find two wolves essentially flanking me. Not any two wolves. The obnoxious one. And the shy one.

I had hoped I'd seen the last of them.

Or had I? What had possessed me to stay in Creekside and walk into the restaurant I knew was owned by the East Creekside leader's brother, suspecting family might eat there.

I'd been hoping to see the two wolves again.

I grabbed a handful of napkins and started cleaning my mouth. The shy one touched my hand and lowered it away from my face. He lingered on my wrist.

"Don't do that," he said. "I like the color on your lips."

Jeezus.

My cock woke right the fuck up. I inhaled, clearing the scent of blood from my nostrils. Arousal. The scent emanating from the two Alphas hung heavy in the air.

"Do you want another steak?" the obnoxious one asked.

I swallowed hard. "No, thank you ... I'm full."

The shy one. "Not too full, I hope."

The innuendo was obvious. Any more clear and I was going to spill seed in my jeans. This is what I'd been hoping for when I stayed in town. Hadn't thought it would happen.

I wasn't sure what to say next.

"I'm sure there's adequate space," I ventured and blushed—fiercely. I was in unknown territory. Flirting wasn't something I'd had *any* practice in. And this wasn't even that.

These two Alphas wanted to go straight to rutting with me.

When these two wolves piled out of that truck this morning in my driveway, I knew. They were close, I could tell. It was a fantasy of mine. To lose my virginity to two Alphas.

Now that I had them.

I was petrified.

I settled my breathing.

I wanted this.

"Where do we want to go?" I asked.

"We have a cabin," the obnoxious one said. *Bryant.* I might as well use their names. We were about to get much more intimate with each other.

The shy one—Grayson slid from the booth and let me out. He wasn't subtle. He guided me out of the restaurant by placing his hand on the small of my back.

Grayson helped me into the truck, giving me a hoist by cupping my ass. I was sandwiched between the two Alphas on the leather bench seating in the truck's cab.

My cock was already weeping when Grayson cupped my face and brought his lips to mine. He started soft, tentative— then lust took over. He strained at his seatbelt to get closer to me.

Breathing against my lips, his meaty hand traveled to my cock. His palm was warm as he cupped my jeans and used the heel of his hand to caress my stiffening length.

I wasn't sure where we were going as we drove off the road into the forest. I should have cared. I knew nothing about these two wolves. I only knew I wanted them to touch me.

Bryant stopped the truck in front of a shed beside a massive log home. It wasn't the only one. The area was a collective of pack houses. The cabin must be nearby.

Grayson lifted me down from the cab of the truck, pressed my back against the side of the back panel, and possessed my mouth; his hands seeking under my coat. His tongue was forceful and held so much promise. My knees nearly buckled as I groaned; his hand back on my cock.

I caught his scent before I saw him. Bryant placed his hand on Grayson's shoulder. Grayson released my mouth. His desire had blown his pupils wide.

I shivered as Bryant gripped my neck and used the curled fingers of his other hand to lift my chin. His thumb slipped up my chin to my bottom lip. He pulled the plump flesh down, then slipped his thumb into my mouth. He rode it along my tongue. I closed my lips and sucked on it.

I wasn't stupid. I know what it was meant to replicate.

I swirled my tongue around his thumb. My cock pulsed.

I moaned.

"Such a sweet Omega," Bryant said. He withdrew his thumb. I wanted to chase it. To have it fill my mouth again. My desire to be filled was bordering on psychotic.

"This way," Grayson said and headed off across the clearing. We entered the forest. There was a well-worn path but the sun was going down. It would be dark soon. I longed for my wolf eyes. Before we arrived anywhere resembling a cabin, Grayson stopped and returned to my lips.

As he cupped my face and kissed me, Bryant stepped up behind me, trapping me between them. Bryant's hands were busy.

Cold air swirled between my thighs as Bryant unlatched and dropped the bottom half of my clothing around my ankles. My coat and shirt were next. I kicked off my shoes and stepped out of my pants. The cold air only bit my bare skin for a second.

I wrapped my arms around Grayson's neck and returned to his mouth, our intimacy had been interrupted by Bryant's decision to strip me.

Bryant's warm lips and tongue had me moaning as he explored the back of my neck and my shoulders. He sucked and dragged his teeth across my claiming area.

Back up my neck, his hot quick breath pummeled the soft skin behind my ear.

"Jump up," he whispered.

I took that to mean jump onto Grayson. I leaped up and wrapped my legs around Grayson's waist. Bryant growled and his hand traveled down my ribcage to my thigh.

Onto my ass.

I released Grayson's mouth and groaned as Bryant's thick finger circled my hole. He took the glorious sensation away and licked his finger, then returned. He pressed against the resistance.

My cock pulsed. I was smearing Grayson's coat in precum.

"Fuck." I pressed my forehead to Grayson's. No longer content with his finger, Bryant had ducked down and kissed and licked my tailbone.

One hand on each ass cheek, his tongue took over where he'd let off with his finger. Hot and wet, the prodding thickness circled my hole. "Hold him," he said to Grayson.

"Got him."

Getting right underneath me, Bryant attacked my hole with his mouth—his lips—and his tongue. Slurping, licking, and piercing. The lurid sensations made me frantic.

Again—and again, Bryant took me to places that made my mind buzz.

A coil tightened in my gut.

I panted against Grayson's lips.

"Please," I whispered.

"I think he's ready," Grayson said to Bryant.

Bryant rose to his feet. "Set him down." After I was back down on the ground, Bryant turned me to face him. He held my chin. "I want you to taste yourself."

Please.

I gripped his face and kissed him. His lips were musky, warm, and wet. I dove into his mouth, wanting to taste everything. I'd never felt so crazed; every taste and scent brought me to the verge of absolute distraction. Every touch from Bryant had ignited an inferno in me.

I turned back to Grayson. As well as hunger, there was a kindness in his eyes I found appealing. I rose to my toes and brought my lips near his. He inhaled the scent of them before covering them in a tender kiss. I could fall for a wolf like Grayson.

Grayson bent down and picked up my clothes. My clothing gathered he led the way to the cabin. It was old. Like really old. But it was neat and cozy inside. The air was a little chilly. I sat on the bed as the two older wolves fussed over starting a fire in the stone fireplace.

I was conscious of their age. I hadn't been whelped until they were in their late 20s ... maybe even 30s. I studied Grayson as he arranged kindling. He was extreme on the attractive scale. Muscular and gorgeous. Dark blond hair, grey at the temples. And he had the softest grey eyes.

Eyes you could get lost in they were so expressive.

Bryant was in contrast. Same black features as his brother Jonas, but arranged in an almost angry way. Angry *and* beautiful. He scared me a little.

Bryant was the first to approach the bed.

"You still up for this?" he asked me.

I reached between my legs and stroked my hard cock. That was my answer. Bryant focused on what I was doing and licked his lips. He sank to his knees at the edge of the bed and coaxed me forward. I hung my legs over the edge of the bed. I jumped a little as a naked Grayson sat behind me. I was between his thighs. His thick cock lain against my spine; his hands on my shoulders.

He kissed the back of my neck as Bryant sucked my cock into his mouth.

It was more than I had dreamed of. Two wolves. Each doing their best to draw my attention. To make me feel good. I felt cared for. It was an exquisite high.

Bryant sucked and pumped, giving my slit special attention. His focus was on tasting everything. Grayson just wanted to be near me. On my neck and shoulders—on my lips.

Grayson shuffled back. He and Bryant had communicated something. We were changing up our positions. Grayson lifted me and tossed me toward the head of the bed.

I landed with a bounce.

It made me smile. I liked being thrown around.

I tucked a pillow under my head.

Bryant stood and removed his clothes. My cock pulsed. Grayson had been behind me. I hadn't seen him yet. What stood before me was perfection. I whimpered as Bryant approached the bed.

Grayson moved to the foot of the bed.

I pried my gaze away from Bryant to look at Grayson. Where Bryant was covered in black hair, Grayson had pale red and silver hair all over his luscious body.

They were both mouth-watering.

Bryant was back between my legs. This time with his thick rough fingers. He pushed his thumb inside me. I adjusted to the intrusion. When he withdrew his thumb, a rivulet of wetness ran from my hole to my tailbone. I'd never been this wet before.

I was aching for them.

Both of them.

Bryant shoved my legs apart and hovered above me. One hand beside my head, the other guiding his cock, he kissed me as he pushed past my tight virginal ring.

I mewled against his mouth, fighting to relax. The burn was incredible. I regretted not splurging and ordering some dildos to practice with.

He thrust higher.

I squeaked out a whimper.

Bryant released my lips.

"You're all right," he whispered. "Breathe."

I felt a hand slip into mine. Grayson. He held my hand.

"If you want me to stop," Bryant said. "I will."

I shook my head. "No … please no."

Bryant sat back on his haunches and grasped my thighs. He rocked his hips forward. This angle was easier on me. I groaned and threw my head back as he fully seated himself in me.

"Beautiful Omega." Grayson stroked my face and leaned over me.

And kissed me.

Bryant started thrusting, his cock dragging back and forth against a sensitive area inside my hole. I couldn't pick a focus as my ass warmed and Bryant's rhythm set my body alight.

I grasped Grayson's face and kept his lips on mine.

I *could* focus on both at once. Bryant filling my lust-driven hole and Grayson quenching my need for intimate affection. I hummed against Grayson's mouth, my body rocking up and down against the bed. First slow—then faster. Bryant was grunting.

"*So* beautiful," Grayson whispered as Bryant's thrusts turned jarring. He lifted my legs. Grayson moved back. Slamming into me, Bryant howled softly and closed his eyes.

His thrusting slowed. Just a hard push every few seconds. I touched my stomach. Being filled with his seed didn't feel any different. It wasn't until he retreated that I felt the trickle of what he had left in me. He climbed off the bed and wandered toward the kitchen.

I smiled.

And then, there he was.

Grayson.

My hole was stretched but Grayson's thick cock still met some resistance. He was gentle and slow. Pumping and thrusting as he watched my eyes. I touched his face. He angled his cheek into my palm and rubbed his face against my skin. He turned his face and kissed my hand.

This felt different than with Bryant.

Bryant was all business.

This meant more to Grayson.

I wrapped my legs around his waist as he tugged me into an embrace in his strong and protective arms. He nuzzled my neck as he pumped into me, his hips undulating.

A short shiver and he stopped moving

He pulled me tighter to him and groaned in my ear.

A few slow thrusts of his hips and I knew he was filling me.

I almost teared up when he whispered, "My precious Omega," in my ear.

The moment was interrupted by Bryant bouncing back onto the bed. He lay down beside me and tucked a pillow under his head. Grayson flopped down on the other side of me.

I exhaled.

I felt vulnerable without his body on top of mine.

I turned to face Grayson and tucked my forehead up against his shoulder. I clung to his bicep. Bryant moved closer to me and fitted my ass against the curve of his groin. He kissed the back of my neck and put his hand on my hip. He stroked his thumb back and forth across my skin.

I closed my eyes.

I could sleep like this but the bed wasn't made for three wolves.

"I can shift and find my way back to my car," I said.

Grayson lifted his head. "Are you sure? One of us can drive you."

I sat up. "I need the fresh air to clear my head."

"You're not regretting this, are you?" Bryant said.

I put my hand on Bryant's hand and smiled at him. "Not at all."

"We'd like to see you again," Grayson said. I wasn't going to question his assumption when it came to what Bryant wanted. Maybe they'd done this before.

"I'll have to check my calendar. Gotta paint that church, you know."

Bryant snorted out a laugh.

Grayson gave me a gentle smile that reached his eyes. It was breathtaking. I couldn't help myself. I leaned down and kissed him. I needed to memorize the feel of his lips so I could replay the sensation in my mind when thoughts of him inevitably drifted in.

Bryant moved aside so I could get off the bed. In fairness, I kissed him as well. It didn't pull at my gut the way it did when I kissed Grayson.

"I'll stop by next time I'm in town," I said. "I know where you are now."

Grayson frowned at me. "I won't be here. I'm supposed to move out tonight."

"To where?"

"The boarding house," Bryant answered.

I inhaled. "Well, that makes things slightly more complicated."

No, it didn't.

I knew I'd be finding myself on Grayson's doorstep at the boarding house. I could imagine it being just us. Bryant had been fun but I knew who I wanted to be with.

Promises were made to work it out and I dressed and left.

My thoughts were of Grayson.

Of those beautiful grey eyes of his.

And his lips.

God ... his lips.

Chapter Seven | Bryant

I was sad to see Hunter go. It made lying in bed with Grayson naked and freshly rutted awkward. If I'd given Hunter a ride back into town, I could've dropped Grayson off at the boarding house.

It was still early enough to get him there.

"Do you want a ride to the boarding house?"

"Maybe in a few minutes." Grayson closed his eyes. He had to be feeling as weird about this as I did. We had *never* done anything like this before. Not even close.

"Are we going to talk about this?" I asked.

"About what?"

"About bringing an Omega home and rutting with him—together."

"I thought that's what you wanted," Grayson replied.

"I thought that's what *you* wanted."

Grayson layered his arms across his stomach. "You have no idea what I want."

I turned on my side to watch him. "Maybe you should tell me." I touched his arm as a stream of tears escaped from the eye I could see and ended in his ear. "Grayson … what?"

He snuffled and more tears ran down his face. I rose on one elbow. His face was a mess of tears. "Fuck, Grayson. Please tell me what's going on."

My heart thundered. I'd never seen Grayson like this. I didn't like to see him like this. His absolute distress was tearing my soul into little pieces.

"God, Bryant," he wailed and rolled away from me.

I moved closer to him and put my hand on his arm. My heart thundered louder as I leaned forward and kissed his shoulder. He stiffened.

"Don't," he said. "Don't you dare tease me."

I kissed his shoulder again. "I'm not teasing you." I'm not sure what possessed me. Seeing Grayson suffering like that awoke something in me. Something I'd been shoving down.

Grayson rolled onto his back. He reached up and held my face. I wanted to melt into his hand. I hadn't realized how much I'd been craving his touch.

"I'm not teasing you," I repeated.

Grayson stroked my skin with his thumb. "You have no idea how much I love you."

My arm lost its strength to hold me. I tumbled onto the pillow beside Grayson. He took it the wrong way. He rolled away from me and started to leave the bed.

I clamped onto his arm to stop him.

"Don't you dare leave me after a declaration like that."

Grayson sighed.

"Come back," I said. Reluctantly, Grayson lay back on the bed. This time, I wasn't stopping at his shoulder. I wrapped my hand around the back of his neck and eased him toward me.

"What …?" he whispered.

"Shh." I brought our foreheads together. Grayson's breathing was hot and short. At this distance, Grayson's scent filled my senses. With a need I hadn't known I'd been harboring, I tasted Grayson's lips for the first time. I never wanted to be without them again.

Grayson hesitated at first, then cupped my face and deepened the kiss. Alternated deepening and hesitation. A mix of desperation and fear. He didn't trust what I was feeling.

I separated our lips. Kept them close enough that our upper lips were still in contact. I didn't want to be away from them. "What do you need to hear from me?"

"I need to know what you're *really* feeling. We just rutted with a beautiful Omega. You could be riding on the high of that still."

That Omega had nothing on this Alpha. I brushed my fingers through the hair above his ear. Grayson was pure. Perfect, gentle, and pure. I'd never met someone as soft-spoken as him. Someone whose eyes spoke more than his mouth ever had. Grayson had a good heart. He was caring and loyal. I had endeavored to give him a good life. He deserved it.

Two months ago, I had brought him the idea of staying out of wolf form for a while. Told him I needed a break. That was partially true. I needed a break, not from wolf life. I loved wolf life. I needed a break from the silence between us when we couldn't speak.

I stroked his cheek. I had needed to hear his voice.

"Bryant?"

I licked my lips and licked his in the process. I needed some reassurance. I slipped my tongue between his lips and kissed him. Just soft and quick. The closeness with him was all I needed.

"I love you too," I whispered.

Grayson groaned and attacked my mouth. Pushed me onto my back and straddled my thighs. Both of his hands held my face as his lips chased the words I had spoken.

My heart sang with the release of the sudden confession. I hadn't realized they were there. Those deep feelings. I had never put a word to how I felt about Grayson.

When he'd used the word *love* … everything fell into place. That's why I had collapsed. I *wasn't* surprised to hear him utter those words. I'd suspected something was going on with him. I *was* surprised at how my body and mind had reacted.

The rush of love I'd felt.

Grayson layered himself on me as I pulled him to me and wrapped my arms around him. I needed him close. One hand on his lower back—the other around the back of his neck.

We were enraptured with each other. Gentle steady kisses like we needed to enjoy every single one as if it would be our last. Grayson thrust against me. Our cocks hardened.

The reality of our potential mating nearly spun me out.

I rolled until Grayson was beneath me and undulated my hips, making him moan and grasp my shoulders. He brought his hips up to meet each thrust of mine.

Our cocks fought for space between us. My foreskin rolled up and back over my cockhead. Our skin became slick and I nearly saw red, my emotions had become so carnal.

Grayson growled and grabbed my ass, guiding me to increase my pace. I felt a howl building in me. I silenced it. We couldn't be heard. The pack would know. This had to be kept a secret.

I concentrated on Grayson's mouth instead and his hard, muscular body beneath me, squirming and thrusting, and running his cock up and down the length of mine.

He grunted and jutted his chin up. I kept my mouth on his and absorbed every seductive sound rumbling from his throat as he spilled seed onto our skin.

My cock slid through his gift and added my own. This bonded us. We'd whispered words of love and we'd spilled seed together. We'd stopped short of claiming and mating.

That would be a step for another day. Tonight, I was going to enjoy what we *had* done. How this was going to change our lives. How Grayson was mine now. And I was his.

I moved off him and pulled him into my arms. He lay his head on my chest and his hand on my stomach. His fingers played with the mess we had left behind between us.

"I love you," Grayson whispered and kissed my cheek.

"I love you too."

There—a second time. This time more clearly. We were in love. I had an incredible wolf in my arms and we were in love. I furrowed my brow. An Alpha wolf.

It deflated my elation, thinking about the reality that we couldn't let anyone know. Even though Lucas said he wouldn't judge—others might.

Jonas had likely told Lucas already that we had led a young Omega out of the restaurant reeking of arousal. I wasn't sure what Lucas would make of that. Five years together— maybe it was a habit of ours. He might think that. He might suspect other things.

I lay my hand along Grayson's jawline and kissed his head.

"Are you still going to move out?"

"I think it might look better."

My heart sank into my stomach. He was right. Two Alphas sharing a small cabin with one bed for any length of time would draw attention. I hugged him to me.

"You'll visit me some nights?" I couldn't visit Grayson at the boarding house. Show up there and stay for hours—maybe overnight. Mama would report our obviously conjugal visits to Lucas.

"Of course." He kissed my jaw and rubbed his lips along it. "I should go."

No.

I whimpered and tears ran down my cheeks.

"This is going to be agony for me," I admitted. "Having you leave now."

"I'll come back tomorrow night. Stay until morning. I need to secure that room tonight. Otherwise I wouldn't be going anywhere." His hand wandered to my chest and stopped above my heart. "Now that I know you love me … things will change between us."

"We can't let anyone know."

"I know." Grayson smiled against my cheek. "I'll try to keep my loving looks in check."

"Only in public. I want plenty of those looks in private."

"I'll store them up for you." Grayson sat up and rose from the bed. This pivotal experience was coming to an end. I reached for him. He responded with a kiss on my outstretched fingers.

His body disappearing behind clothes sent my heart into palpitations. I didn't want to let him go. But I knew I needed to. It was so maddening and heartbreaking that I felt like howling.

I packed the impulse down deep inside.

I joined Grayson at the end of the bed, pulling on clothes so we could head into town. He gathered up what few other shirts and pants he had pilfered from the cabin's shelves.

The drive into town was silent. We had no idea what to say to each other. If either of us had been an Omega, we would be celebrating right now. Letting the rest of the pack know.

Rejoicing in our love.

I pulled up outside the boarding house. I placed my hand on Grayson's and squeezed it. I didn't dare kiss him. He mouthed, "I love you," then left the cab of my truck.

A vacuum sucked every will to live out of my body.

I was in tears as I drove home. I could barely see the road. I wanted to turn around. Turn around and tell the world to be damned. That I had uncovered a level of love I didn't even know was there. That I would do anything to be with this Alpha. Even endure a shunning.

I stopped the truck halfway up the driveway and stared at the trees through the windshield. I might be willing to go through being disgraced but I would never put Grayson through that.

I restarted my way up to Lucas' house, parked outside, and headed for the cabin. It was lonely and cold inside without Grayson there. I inhaled the faint lingering scent of him. It would be hard to sleep on sheets that carried the combined scent of our seed.

I stripped out of my clothes and immersed myself in the bedding that had held us. I caught the scent of Hunter mixed with Grayson's on the pillow beside mine. I'd almost forgotten he'd been here with us tonight. That we had rutted with Hunter together. I smoothed the fabric of the pillowcase with my hand. I liked their combined scent. It was woodsy and soothing.

My mind wandered between *my* experience with Grayson and me watching Grayson rut with Hunter. Grayson thrusting his hips, filling Hunter, and Hunter moaning and mewling.

My cock throbbed.

I dismissed it. Grayson and I belonged to each other. The longing looks Grayson and Hunter had been giving each other were moot now. It had been impossible not to notice. They'd become lost in each other's eyes. Their kisses had been tender. Emotions had come into play.

Our love had pushed all of that aside.

Or had it?

I held the pillow to my chest and hugged it. I fell asleep like that, my nose tucked against their combined scent. It slowed my mind—dissipated my usual fitful sleep.

I AWOKE SURPRISED I hadn't dreamed of Adam being hauled through the forest by his ankles, battered and bloody. I credited the pillow. It had lulled me.

I headed to Lucas' to check for messages. Maybe someone had phoned last night or early this morning looking to have some painting done. Grayson and I still had some flyers to deliver to the outlying residential areas. We could do that today. Maybe along the secluded roads, we could stop the truck and immerse ourselves in each other again.

My body hummed with excitement at the prospect.

I let myself into Lucas' house. The first two times knocking had been a formality. As Lucas' brother, I was family and family didn't need to knock.

I walked straight into a fray of pups. Some leaped up on me. Some backed off and growled at me. A young male out of wolf form of about 6 or 7 approached.

He crossed his arms. "Who are you?"

It must be Lucas' eldest.

"I'm your sire's brother, Bryant."

"What's your business here?"

I smiled. This one was an Alpha leader in the making. His little face looked very stern. Lucas must be very proud of him. "I've come to check the answering machine for messages."

"Those are my sire's messages."

"Some of them might be for me."

He scowled at me. "Why?"

Wow, this pup was intense.

"Because I started a painting business and gave your sire's number on the flyer."

The pup grunted. I tried not to laugh.

"I'm assuming you had his permission."

"I knew he wouldn't mind."

Adam strode into the front hall and placed his hand on the pup's shoulder. "Stop running an interrogation on your sire's brother. He has a legitimate reason to be here ... he's family."

"He used the business phone number," the pup argued.

"And Lucas didn't mind." Adam looked at me. "You have a message waiting."

That got my blood bubbling. First day out of the gate and we might have a job. A quick trip to the hardware store and we'd be set. Grayson and I could spend the day working together.

And tonight ... he'd be back in my arms.

"Bryant, could I speak with you, please." Lucas stood at the end of the hallway. "In private."

Adam was wrong. It seemed Lucas *had* been upset about us using his phone number. Now, he was going to ream me out for assuming we could. I followed him down the hall to his office.

Once inside, Lucas closed the door and leaned against it. There would be no escaping if he became aggressive. I prepared myself for the discussion about to unfold.

"I happened to look out my front window last night," Lucas started.

Okay. Not what I was expecting. I was in trouble but not for using the phone number.

"Sorry about that," I replied. "We should have waited until we got back to the cabin."

"You were practically rutting with him on the driveway in front of my house. Young pups are living here. What if they had seen you thumb rutting that wolf's mouth? Or Grayson groping him."

I looked at the floor. "I'm sorry. I really am. We were caught up in the moment."

My ears burned as my face flushed. We hadn't been thinking. We'd been riding the high of arousal, oblivious to our surroundings. The young wolf's scent had been intoxicating.

"I didn't recognize him," Lucas said.

"He's from Riverton. Hunter."

"What was he doing in Creekside?"

" He works here sometimes. Painting."

"You compete with him?" His voice escalated. "Is this a new thing with my brothers?" He strode closer to me. "Rutting, mating, and claiming your competitors?"

I looked up at Lucas. "But ... you and Adam?"

"Not the same. We waited until the pull was undeniable. Is he fated to either of you?"

"It's not like that. Neither of us is planning on forming a mating bond with him."

"And that's the other thing." Lucas stepped toward me. "You were *both* on him. Is this a routine of yours and Grayson's? Lure a young wolf home with you and rut with him together?"

"Last night was the first time."

Lucas shook his head. "You spent 5 years together. What changed last night?"

"I don't know. We walked into *Growlers* and he was there. The rest just unfolded."

"You both rutted with him?"

The blush crept further. Down my throat and neck. It prickled my skin. As pack leader, Lucas had every right to ask me these questions. My mind jerked and bucked to defy him.

"It didn't feel wrong."

"Maybe not, but this is not the kind of behavior I want to see in the pack. An Alpha with two Omegas is acceptable. This is *not*. As my brother, you should know this."

I felt like weeping. Not only was I in love with another Alpha male but there was an Omega out there I suspected Grayson had feelings for. It was an untenable situation we were in.

I almost felt like running off into the forest away from everyone. Grayson would have Hunter, an Omega, and the complication of our love for each other could be forgotten.

"Bryant."

Lucas was waiting for a reply. I only had one.

"I can't promise it won't happen again." It was the truth. I didn't want to run away. I wanted to fight for my love for Grayson. I wanted to keep giving Grayson what he desired.

"I don't understand. What am I missing?"

"I disagree with the prejudice."

Lucas' brow dipped. "You can't disagree with a prejudice … it just exists."

"Then I'm willing to go against it."

"The two of you are going to continue rutting with this Hunter?"

"Maybe."

Lucas groaned. "You're arguing with me over something that might not even happen?"

"I haven't asked Grayson what he wants yet." After exchanging words of love, I wondered if Grayson would feel differently about rutting with the Omega again.

Maybe.

I wasn't sure.

Lucas just shook his head. "Did Grayson move into the boarding house?"

"He did."

"Mama won't tolerate the two of you bringing that wolf back there."

"We wouldn't dare."

"Here in the cabin, there will be no howling from the three of you."

I nodded. "Of course." It wasn't permission from Lucas but it was an agreement to turn a blind eye to our transgression. It was the best I could hope for. "Can I go now?"

"You'll need to collect your message. Sounds like a good job." Lucas turned to the desk and lifted a slip of paper. "I've written down the details. You can use the phone to call him back."

I was able to refocus as Lucas left the office. It *was* a good job. Painting the three upstairs bedrooms of a house along the main street. Hunter must be too busy with the church.

Chapter Eight | Grayson

I was barely awake when someone knocked on the door to my suite. I pulled on some pants and stumbled to answer it. It was Mama.

"There's someone here to see you," she said. "Should I send him up?"

Bryant.

I inhaled the air.

Not Bryant but my stomach still tumbled, giddy.

"Sure, he can come up."

I found a shirt and finished dressing. When I turned around, Hunter was standing in the doorway. He was chewing on his bottom lip. I wanted to take over and taste it for myself.

"I wasn't sure whether to come," he said.

"You weren't sure I'd be moved in?"

"I wasn't sure if you'd want to see me."

"Come in and close the door."

Hunter crept in a couple of steps and shut the door behind him. His gaze went from my face to my body and back again. He stuffed his hands in his coat pockets.

"Why weren't you sure?' I asked.

"Because you're alone. You're not with Bryant."

"Why would that stop you?" I wanted to know where he thought this was going. Now that Bryant and I were together, my desire for Hunter had changed.

I sighed.

Or had it?

"Because I don't know if that's the way you usually do things. Always together."

"We'd never done that before."

Hunter's eyes opened wide and he stared at me. "Really? Me either."

"You seemed to be comfortable with it."

Hunter took a step toward me. "*You* made me feel comfortable."

"Bryant a bit intense for you?"

His brow dipped. "Yes, but, no ... I felt a *connection* with you."

My chest tightened and my breathing became shallow. My heart thundered. I'd felt it too. Not fated mate strong but something close to it. I would fight anyone who approached him.

Except Bryant.

Last night in bed together, just the two of us, me and Bryant, our friendship had transformed into something unexpected and glorious. We had a shared love between us now.

But earlier in the night, our bodies moving together with Hunter as three had felt like the most natural thing in the world. I wandered closer to him. He was truly a beautiful Omega.

His scent crawled through my senses, tripping off every single wire. Bryant wouldn't deny me this one taste. I cupped Hunter's face and quenched my absolute need for him.

Hunter slung his arms around my neck as our lips became reacquainted. I lifted him so his legs were wrapped around my waist. I wouldn't let this go any further.

Not without talking to Bryant first.

"I want you," Hunter whispered against my lips.

I lowered him to the ground. "It's not that easy."

Hunter whined. "Why?"

The three of us had shared something incredible last night. Hunter hadn't felt like a casual rut. We were in this together. Whatever *this* was. I could tell him our secret.

"After you left, I told Bryant I'm in love with him."

"Oh." Hunter placed his hand on my chest. "And what did he say?"

"That he loves me too."

Hunter pressed his lips together and released them with a pop. He stepped away from me. "And you claimed and mated with each other."

"No." I shook my head. "We're not there yet."

"Why did you kiss me just now?"

I'd been turning that over in my mind. Bryant and I could have claimed each other last night. Something hadn't felt complete. Now I knew the answer why.

"You might be the reason we're not there yet."

Hunter crossed his arms. "What does that mean?"

I was distracted by the scent I *had* been expecting this morning. I walked to the door and let him in. He was musky, gorgeous, and we were in love. I longed to be in his arms again.

Bryant's eyebrows rose when he saw Hunter standing in the middle of the room.

"Early morning visitor?" he asked.

"We had things to talk about," I replied.

"Such as?"

"Such as this." I stepped close to Hunter, held his face in both hands, and settled a kiss on the young Omega meant to make him crumple at the knees.

"Fuck," Bryant whispered beside me and touched my shoulder. I backed away. My breath caught as Bryant took my place. Hunter rose on his toes and welcomed Bryant's mouth to his.

I groaned as I watched them immerse themselves in each other.

Bryant broke the kiss and turned to me. He shifted his attention from Hunter. His lips were warm and wet, carrying the scent of Hunter, as he caressed his mouth against mine.

Hunter's hands were in the mix. I kissed Hunter again. Then Bryant did as he angled Hunter toward the bed, stepping him back. He lifted Hunter and threw him onto the bed, and growled.

I was right behind him.

Hunter's clothes didn't stand a chance. We hauled off his jeans and exposed his hard cock. The head was plump and glistening. I let Bryant suck the precum away, then took over, diving onto Hunter's length. Bryant gripped and pumped the base of Hunter's cock as I bobbed.

I sucked it from root to tip. Bryant crowded in and ran his lips along one side. I took the other so our lips would meet. Our lips joined, we caressed Hunter's entire cock with our lips and tongues.

Hunter dug his fingers into our hair and groaned. His ass muscles clenched. Bryant took over sucking his cock deep into his throat and I moved to Hunter's balls. They were firm and pink, covered in the most delicate fuzz. I wet the tiny hairs, then sucked a sac into my mouth.

Hunter whined and squirmed. I cupped his other ball in my hand and stroked the stretch of skin between his balls and his hole.

"God … please," Hunter said, probably louder than he should.

I dropped his thoroughly tongue-caressed ball from my mouth and pressed my finger against Hunter's hole. Then two. He panted, his hole tightening and releasing.

I pushed two fingers into him and found my mark. The sensitive button that would take him up into an ecstatic upward spiral. His hips jerked as I ran my pads over it.

A few rhythmic taps and his hold on my hair turned into a vicious pull.

"Fuck," he gasped.

Bryant hummed to increase the intensity of the sensation we were bringing him. Hunter's hole clamped on my fingers. Hunter whimpered and thrust his hips up.

The scent of his seed filled my nostrils.

After a few clamping sensations around my fingers, Hunter's body stilled. I withdrew them and turned Bryant's face to me. I knew he would have saved some for me.

Bryant kissed me and pushed my share of Hunter's seed against my tongue. We reveled in experiencing it together, giving and taking, enjoying every drop.

Hunter sat up and touched our shoulders.

Bryant was the first to kiss him. The three of us were sharing in the pleasure. Hunter searched my mouth when he kissed me. For a brief moment, all three of us were kissing each other.

This felt right.

Hunter belonged to us.

I pulled away from the kiss.

And we belonged to him. I kissed the side of his neck. Bryant the other. Hunter tipped his head backward and gripped us by the back of our necks.

Slow and with ceremony, Bryant removed Hunter's coat. I removed his shirt. Hunter's chest bare, we ran our lips halfway to Hunter's shoulders.

"Yes, please yes," Hunter whispered. "I'm yours."

Bryant growled first, then uttered the words, "I'm yours."

I kissed Hunter's shoulder. "I'm yours."

Bryant sank his teeth into Hunter's flesh a brief moment before me. Hunter cried out and clung to us both. My cock throbbed, wanting to sink into my Omega and plant my seed. In tandem, Hunter's blood filled my mouth. Then the buzz of his consciousness appeared just out of reach.

In unison, Bryant and I released him and slipped off our shirts. Hunter with blood dripping down his arms and chest, positioned himself, kneeling. The smell of iron permeated the air.

I was the first he claimed. I snapped into his mind when he invited me in. He wanted me to be there with him when he bit Bryant. A wave of love for me rolled over me as Hunter bit down and claimed Bryant. I half expected Bryant's inner voice to join us. It didn't.

It was shimmering in the distance but I couldn't get in.

We pulled away from each other in a stupor. There would be no hiding now. The smell of blood coming from my suite had to be detectable. I was drunk with it.

Soon Lucas would know what we'd done.

Hunter stroked his hands through our hair. "Your claiming should be private."

"But you're one with us," Bryant argued.

"Private," Hunter repeated. "Mate with the love of your life." He smiled at us. He'd accessed our love for each other. "I'll be around. Call me when you've had your time together."

"Church to paint?" Bryant cocked his head to one side.

Hunter snorted. "Something like that. Gonna have trouble lifting my arms to paint." He touched either side of his neck as if to check and make sure he'd truly been claimed.

Bryant closed his eyes and frowned. A few changes of expression then he opened them and sighed. "Lucas has a lot of questions."

"What are you going to tell him?" I asked.

"The truth." Bryant lowered his head onto Hunter's lap. "You're *our* Omega now."

Hunter placed his hand on Bryant's head. "My Alpha." He used his other hand to cradle my face. I leaned into his touch. "My Alpha." His smile was precious. "My perfect Alphas."

I longed to continue. To hold each other, get lost in each other's eyes, and touch and taste every morsel of flesh between us. Mate with our Omega until we could no longer breathe.

I groaned.

Her scent outside the door was overpowering.

Mama was angry.

Her hammering on the door disrupted the sweet seductive unity we'd been sharing. Bryant was first to his feet. He handed Hunter his pants from off the floor.

"Just a second," I shouted and waited for Hunter to dress. After he was for the most part decent, I opened the door. Mama's nose twitched as she entered the room.

"I've told Lucas I smelled blood," she said.

I looked over my shoulder. Two crimson spots were forming on Hunter's white t-shirt. Bryant and I were shirtless. It was obvious what had happened.

Mama's eyes widened after surveying the room. "*What* have you done?"

"I've claimed my Omega," I answered.

Bryant crossed his arms. "So have I."

Hunter climbed off the bed. He came to my side, one arm around my waist, his head on my shoulder. Bryant stepped in beside our sweet Omega and put his arm around us both.

We were three wolves—on the precipice of being mated.

Chapter Nine | Hunter

I had started at the front peak of the church. Thankfully, I only needed a ladder to reach it. I would have had to hire someone to construct my scaffolding for me. It wasn't a job for one. Or I could have asked my Alphas to do it for me. They had offered to help me get started on my job.

My face stretched into a giddy smile. I'd been claimed this morning in the most unconventional situation I'd ever heard of. There were stories of two Alpha males forming a mated pair but they always lived their lives as wolves off in the wilderness.

Grayson and Bryant were in love and living their lives out of wolf form. And they'd claimed me as their Omega. We'd form a family. I'd bear their pups someday.

I refocused on what I was doing. The fresh coat of white paint was making a difference. The pastor had told me it had been 15 years since the church was painted last. I painted five more slats and then moved down the ladder. I lowered my arm to give it a rest. This was going to take longer than usual. My trapezius muscles were aching. They'd both bitten down hard.

"Hey, Hunter!"

I looked down the ladder and smiled. "Hey!" Three of my friends from Riverton were standing at the base of the ladder, staring up at me, including my roommate Daniel.

I set my paintbrush on the paint can, and clattered down the ladder. I leaped the last two steps onto the ground. "What are you all doing here?"

"Thought we'd check out what's happening in Creekside," Daniel said. "You seem enamored with the place. Here two days in a row."

I hitched my thumb at the church. "I have jobs here."

"And you stayed here after your job yesterday … because you were hungry. Until late." Daniel crossed his arms. "We have a restaurant in Riverton. Spill. You've met someone."

I couldn't contain the grin that sprung out on my face. "Maybe."

My best friend Peter shoved my shoulder. "We knew it."

I slipped my coat and shirt off one side, exposing one bite mark. That's all they were getting from me. They'd find out some other time I'd been claimed by *two* Alphas.

Peter coughed out a gleeful laugh. "On, my god … you've been claimed? Who is it? You have to tell us who it is! Is he your fated mate?"

"Not fated, no. Close to it. There was a definite pull between us." I rolled my eyes. "Oh, my god … he's incredible. Big. Strong … gorgeous. A perfect Alpha."

"What's his name?"

The three of us had discussed this. In public Grayson was my Alpha. I was his claimed Omega. Bryant would retain his position as Grayson's best friend. Bryant had asked Lucas to keep Mama's report of our claiming from the pack until we had a chance to explain ourselves to him.

That meeting was set for tonight.

After that, Grayson would move back in with Bryant.

Mama had predictably tossed him out.

"His name is Grayson."

I would have been just as happy to play Bryant's Omega. I knew Bryant would grow on me. He was intense but he was kind. And loving. The depth of his love for Grayson was stunning.

"Grayson is a powerful name."

I groaned. "So powerful. The first time we rutted, it blew my world wide open."

I could see Daniel was containing himself. He wanted to tease me. Instead, he asked me a serious question. He cared about me. We'd lived together for 3 years.

"He was your first rut?"

Not technically. Bryant had rutted with me first. Grayson had been so much sweeter. His motions had felt more like the mating of two fated mates. I considered him my first.

I gave a partial answer.

"I knew he was the one from the first moment I set eyes on him."

"When did you meet him?"

I pulled my lips into my mouth. This was going to be embarrassing.

"Yesterday morning," I replied.

"Wow." Peter stepped back. My third friend Eric's eyes grew wide.

"I know. It was quick."

"And he's not your fated mate," Daniel said.

I shook my head. "Like I said. I just knew."

"When do we get to meet him?" Peter asked.

I looked up along the road a short way. I'd caught their combined scent. Grayson's was faint but it was imprinted in my memory. I could pull it out of the air. We'd arranged to meet for a midday feed. Just my luck, my entire group of friends would be there when they arrived.

I must have been staring because my three friends turned to see what I was looking at. As three Omegas, their scent changed. My two Alphas were ominous. They'd elicited a fear response from my friends. That made me feel proud. Proud and protected.

"Hunter," Grayson said as he put his arm around my shoulders. "Who do we have here?"

"My reprobate group of friends." I pointed at each in turn. "Peter, Daniel, and Eric. Daniel is my roommate. We've all known each other since high school."

"The insane colors on your house don't bother you?" Bryant asked Daniel.

"You've seen the house?" Daniel asked.

"We bought Hunter's old van," Grayson answered. "I don't mind the house."

"Oh … um, no," Daniel answered Bryant. I'd told him an older obnoxious wolf and shy wolf had bought my van. He'd probably worked out which was which.

"Are we going for a feed?" Bryant asked. "I'm starving."

"You're always hungry," Grayson said.

"That's because I know how to work," Bryant replied.

"Are you saying I don't?"

"You're so damned fussy."

"That's because I want to do a good job."

Jeezus.

They were like an old mated couple. I turned and patted Grayson's chest. Grayson inhaled a long breath. He made eye contact with each of my friends. "It was nice to meet you all."

"Yeah," Bryant said. "It's nice meeting Hunter's friends."

I looked at my friends. "We'll finish this debrief later?" They would want more details. How I'd gone from selling my van to being claimed in one day for example.

"We'll talk when you emerge," Peter said.

My friends were expecting that Grayson and I would spend the next 10 days mating, trying for a pup. That wasn't the plan. Tonight we were meeting with Lucas. Later in the night Grayson and Bryant would be claiming and mating with each other. I'd join them the following night.

We'd be back at work the next morning.

The three of us couldn't disappear for 10 days to mate.

As we walked down the street, I so badly wanted to hold both their hands. I had to be content to hold Grayson's alone. Grayson guided me into the restaurant, his hands on both my shoulders.

I'd never have to worry about a human calling me a *faggot* ever again.

Both Grayson and Bryant would rip anyone who tried to hurt me to shreds. It gave me a new confidence. I stood straighter. We took a seat at the booth at the back of the restaurant.

Grayson's arm was back around my shoulders.

The brother of Bryant's who owned the restaurant tipped his head to one side as he approached the booth. "Do we have something to celebrate today?"

"Jonas," Bryant said. "I want you to meet Hunter. Grayson's Omega."

"You work quick." Jonas set one hand on his hip. "You've only been here a few days."

"When you know, you know," Grayson replied and tugged me closer to him.

"Fated?" Jonas asked.

"No, but I think the universe might have chosen him for me."

I smiled. That was the sweetest thing I had ever heard. I leaned my head against Grayson's shoulder. I would do anything for this wolf.

Even share him.

I looked at Bryant and smiled.

Grayson's statement of the universe choosing me had pleased Bryant. Jonas would have to be blind to miss the loving gaze Bryant and Grayson were giving each other.

Jonas cleared his throat.

"Anything else I should know?"

Bryant looked at Jonas. "Nothing the three of us want to announce."

My heart thundered in my chest. Bryant had strongly hinted to his brother that we were all together. He must trust Jonas to keep our secret. My warm feelings for Bryant increased.

My Alpha was proud to be with Grayson and me.

"I'd like a bison steak," I said to redirect the conversation. It was the surest way to get a raw piece of meat. My stomach was fussy. Cooked meat didn't agree with it.

"A plump beef roast for both of us," Bryant said pointing between him and Grayson.

Grayson grunted. I wasn't sure if that meant he liked Bryant ordering for him or if he was annoyed by it. His relaxed grip around my shoulders told me he wasn't upset.

Jonas nodded his head and wandered off.

Grayson didn't think there was anything strange about Bryant ordering. My two Alphas had been together for 5 years. They'd developed their own routine. Little nuances. I would need to fit in with those somehow. We had some communication work ahead of us.

Might as well start now. They must be nervous about tonight. After all of those years together, they had finally spoken words of love to each other. Tonight would be special.

"You'll be mated soon," I said as quietly as I could.

"About that … we've been talking," Bryant said and reached across the table for my hand. A surge of panic rose in my chest but I let him take it. Only Jonas would be able to see us.

I shoulder-checked.

Jonas *was* watching us.

"We want you to be there," he continued. "To witness our claiming."

Grayson kissed my head and kept his lips on my hair. "You're so special to us."

Bryant brushed his thumb back and forth on my hand. So subtle but so telling. I'd been sheltering a fear that Bryant only claimed me because Grayson wanted it.

I gazed into Bryant's eyes.

There was genuine affection there.

It made my heart stutter a little.

"I'd be honored," I answered.

Bryant smiled at me and released my hand. Grayson hugged me tight against him. Then they went back to gazing into each other's eyes.

To be looked at like that was a dream.

Maybe we'd get there.

"Oh, my god," Jonas said. "You're oozing love all over my table."

Bryant bit his bottom lip, tore his attention away from Grayson, and turned to Jonas.

"Sorry."

"Don't be sorry." Jonas set our plates in front of us. "I'm glad to see you happy, brother. A bit unconventional. But who am I to judge. I mated with a human. I have a human baby."

"It's a secret for now," Bryant said.

"Not if you keep looking at each other like that."

"I can't help it," Bryant said. "He's gorgeous and sweet and perfect."

Jonas snorted out a laugh. "You've got it bad, Alpha." He turned his attention to me. "And you're all right with this? Being a part of the love fest between these two?"

"They're my Alphas now."

Jonas' eyebrows rose and he looked back and forth between Bryant and Grayson. "You both claimed him? How is that going to work?"

Bryant laughed. "I'm not going into details about our mating positions."

Jonas rolled his eyes. "That's not what I meant." He crossed his arms. "What did Lucas say? He hasn't announced anything to the pack."

"We're speaking to him tonight first," Grayson said.

"I do *not* envy you," Jonas said. "Disgruntled pack members broke both of Damon's legs."

Jeezus.

I gripped Grayson's thigh and stared at Bryant. Now I was terrified.

"No one can hurt us," Bryant said to me. "We can deal with the few who might object."

"But …. "

"Shh," Grayson whispered and touched my chin. I melted against his hand as he turned my face and kissed me. I moved my hand to his chest and clung to his shirt.

I had nothing to fear.

"Ugh," Jonas said. "Try to keep it in your pants until you three get home."

I felt drunk when Grayson pulled away. It wouldn't be long until I fell for him completely. Bryant was right. Grayson was perfect.

My gaze drifted to the bloody meat in front of me. My wolf took over. I pounced on the steak with both hands. Saw red. And didn't return to full consciousness until I was finished.

I was surprised when another thick piece of meat dropped onto my plate. Grayson had ripped off a chunk of his roast and given it to me. I growled my thanks.

He really was perfect.

Chapter Ten | Bryant

The three of us held hands, Hunter in the center of the bench seating of my truck, as we approached Lucas' house. Our world was about to change. Whether my brother would decide to inform the pack of our unique relationship, we didn't know for sure.

I stopped the truck.

No one was around. I brought Hunter's face to mine and kissed him. It was long and slow to reassure each other. Hunter faced Grayson next and passed the kiss along.

"Okay," I said to no one in particular.

Grayson was the first to leave the truck. He gripped Hunter's hand and led the way up the steps to the front door. I placed my hand on the handle, took a deep breath, and opened the door.

The house was quiet. The pups must be tucked up for the night.

Lucas was sitting in the living room with a drink in one hand. It was a dark liquid in a crystal glass. Lucas only brought that pungent alcohol out when he was stressed.

Lucas rose to his feet. "What the hell have you done?"

"Started the completion of a mating circle," I answered.

"Started?"

"Grayson and I haven't claimed each other yet."

"And that's something you want to do?"

"We're in love with each other."

Lucas grunted. "I knew something was going on."

"When you asked last … we weren't there yet. It's new."

"As in?"

"We just told each other last night."

"Because of this Hunter?"

It annoyed me the way Lucas referred to our Omega. Like he was some random element to my relationship with Grayson. Lucas had no idea how we felt about Hunter.

"Yes, Hunter was a catalyst. Grayson gained the courage to tell me he loved me after our experience with Hunter. I wasn't far behind. Our honest affection for Hunter changed us."

"You both claimed Hunter?"

"And he claimed us."

"You're that serious about him."

"He belongs with us. He's our Omega."

Lucas sighed. "How the hell am I supposed to spin this?"

"Don't. Just leave us be."

"You belong to a pack."

"We'll be our own pack."

I heard Hunter gasp beside me. It would be new to him but I would never let anyone hurt him. If that meant being our own pack and taking off, I'd be willing to do that.

So would Grayson.

Lucas set his drink down. "Brother. You've only just come back to us."

"I have to consider what's best for my family."

Hunter's hand slipped into mine. Grayson's into the other. I'd spoken the truth. We *were* a family now. We'd stand together against the prejudice.

After what stretched on for nearly 30 seconds, Lucas sniffed and raised his chin. "We can talk more later."

"Alpha."

All three of us backed away from him and scurried out through the front door. On the way, we encountered Adam. He'd been standing outside the living room and listening.

I couldn't read the look he'd given us.

It bothered me, not knowing, even though I'd made my peace with Adam. What he thought about our union would be discussed with Lucas. His input would matter.

I arrived at the cabin first. Grayson and Hunter had stopped to kiss. I smiled. Hunter made Grayson happy. Tonight would be special for all three of us. Once Grayson and I claimed each other, we would both have the opportunity to mate with Hunter as our claimed Omega.

I had the fire started by the time Grayson and Hunter piled through the door, giggling. I'd never seen Grayson so outwardly happy. An inferno of love burned inside for him. He squatted beside me as I fiddled with putting a log on the fire, and kissed the side of my head.

"I love you," he said and kissed me again.

I reached over my shoulder and cupped the back of his neck. "I love you too."

"I'm yours," he started.

I growled and laughed. I rose to my feet, Grayson coming with me. His coat came off first. Then mine. Both landed in a heap. I cradled his face in both hands and kissed him.

His lips were exquisite. Warm and soft, and I could taste Hunter on them. I looked around the room. Hunter had curled up in an old armchair close to the fire to watch us.

Grayson growled and removed my shirt. I came at him fast and knocked him backward onto the bed. His growl turned into a smile with joy reflecting in his soft grey eyes.

He was beautiful.

I undid the buttons of his plaid shirt and he struggled out of it, then wrapped his arms around me. I hovered above him, then descended for a long lingering kiss.

He groaned and slung his legs around my hips. He pulled me tight to him with his heels on my ass. He was already hard. So was I. I thrust against his body, stoking the fire.

Grayson tipped his head back as I moved to his throat. I sucked and nibbled until he squirmed beneath me. I tucked my face behind his ear and inhaled. Grayson had such a faint scent, but here at its source, it was strong and virile. The love of my life was all wolf.

My hands moved between us, fighting with the buttons and zippers keeping our bodies apart. With furious haste, we both battled our way out of our pants and chucked them aside.

Then our bare heated flesh pressed together. I could feel every contour of his body against mine. We fit, the two of us. Our bodies were muscular and hard, but we fit as well as any Alpha and his Omega. What we were doing … there was nothing unnatural about it.

We were in love. The longing to share our bodies was there.

I kissed my way down Grayson's neck to his chest and sucked a fat nipple into my mouth. Between each suck, I flicked it with my tongue. Grayson moaned and thrust his hips up.

I moved to the center of his hairy chest and kissed a line to Grayson's abs. Even as an aging wolf, his stomach was firm and ridged. All the years as a wolf had kept him muscular.

His seeping cock touched the bottom of my chin. I reached for it and grasped it. It was the first time it had ever been in my hand. His cock fit perfectly in my grasp.

I shuffled further down his body and licked his slit. His copious precum was musky and salty. I sucked and licked, coating my mouth and lips. I wanted to taste all of him.

I fed his cock into my mouth, applying the perfect suction. He groaned and jammed his hand into my hair, and clung to it. He rocked his cock into my mouth. I held steady and let him mate with my face. He hammered his hips up and down. I thought he was going to spill his seed.

Grayson slowed his hips and touched my head lightly. I surged back to his mouth. The welcome I received was fierce and urgent. Grayson spread his legs. I felt between them, venturing into his hole. It wasn't as wet as an Omega would be—but it was wet.

That and the mess of precum seeping from my cock, Grayson wouldn't be hurt. He lifted his knees and held them in both hands. I was slow to slide into him.

It was glorious. The feel of his body encasing my cock. I licked my lips and looked into his eyes as I closed in against his ass. His pupils were blown wide and dark. Blinking up at me, his mouth opened in a silent moan. I pulled my cock back and he closed his eyes and groaned.

It was the most exquisite moment of my life.

Bringing the love of my life pleasure.

I thrust back into him. I had to hold back from spilling my seed. I pumped softly. Grayson panted and ran his tongue along his bottom lip as he undulated his hips in rhythm.

His voice was hoarse.

"I'm yours," he whispered.

"I'm yours," I responded.

Chest to chest, I clung to him. He turned his head from me, exposing his claiming area. I inhaled the scent of it and tasted it. It was heady on my tongue.

The urge screamed up through my body and I bit down.

Grayson howled and cried out in one combined sound. Not loud. Just enough volume to fill the room. He was a claimed wolf. I would be next.

After filling my mouth with his blood, I released him and looked down at him. He was crying. Not tears of pain. Tears of elation. He smiled up at me. His voice buzzed at the edge of my mind.

I watched the changing expression on his face as I set a steady pace in and out of him. Every thrust filled me with emotion. Grayson was about to become my mate.

My balls tightened and I could feel the base of my cock swell. I jammed my knot inside him, stretching him wide. I continued with small movements as release built in me.

I groaned as my knot relaxed and I filled my Alpha with seed. I slid in and out of his slick hole while Grayson held my face and kissed me. Then he pulled my face away from him.

The look on his face turned animalistic. He growled and tossed me off him. I rolled onto my stomach. I wanted to feel him covering my back; his lips on the back of my neck.

He leaped on me, his chest on my back, his cock riding the crease of my ass. I groaned and snarled as he snuffled and nibbled at the back of my ear. I separated my legs and tipped my ass. Grayson's arm pressed against my inner thigh. Without missing a beat, his cock slid home.

My world exploded.

Every desire I'd ever had paled in comparison to the reality of this union. I never knew I had wanted something so much. Grayson guided my arms to be above my head. He held them in place with strong hands as he drilled into me. There was nothing gentle about his desire to claim me.

I growled and met each thrust.

His abs undulated against my ass. Drops of sweat dripped on my shoulder blades.

I had to take a deep breath to speak.

"I'm yours," I managed.

"I'm yours," Grayson growled.

He let me lower one arm. His hot breath was on my neck. His tongue licked a line from my neck to my shoulder, then back again to my claiming area.

I whimpered as he bit down.

A whirlwind hit me as his mind opened to me.

His love and desire for me washed over me.

Grayson's thrusts slowed but pierced higher. He released me from his bite and wrapped his arms around my chest. He kissed the back of my neck as he crested and filled me.

It took us a minute to recover, heaving and sighing.

Grayson rolled off my back. I turned on my side to face him.

Bryant: *"My mate. My Alpha."*

Grayson: *"My love. Mate. And Alpha."*

I looked toward the end of the bed. Hunter was still sitting in the armchair, watching us. He smiled at me. I opened a link with him.

"Bryant: *"Come to bed with us."*

Grayson joined us.

Grayson: *"We need you with us."*

Hunter unfolded himself and discarded his clothing. He crawled up between us from the bottom of the bed. He was quick to cling to Grayson. I tucked his back against my chest.

I kissed his shoulder.

"My sweet Omega," Grayson said and kissed Hunter.

"My Alpha," Hunter whispered.

Their words of affection warmed me. I inhaled the combined scent of them. Hunter reached back and put his hand on my thigh and pulled me tight to him.

"Omega," Grayson whispered. "I want to fill you with pups."

I could feel Hunter's breathing change. His breath hitched before he spoke.

"I would love that," he said at last.

I could see Grayson raise his hand and brush the hair above Hunter's ear.

"I love you, Omega," Grayson said.

My breath escaped in a long gust and my heart tripped around in my chest. Love. In such a short time. The universe had truly brought Hunter to my mate.

I smiled against Hunter's shoulder, lay my hand on Grayson's, still on the side of Hunter's head, and rubbed my lips against Hunter's skin.

I'd never been happier. My Alpha was in the throes of love. He was claimed, mated, and fulfilled. Tears ran from my eyes as I pressed my face to Hunter's flesh.

I sobbed myself to sleep.

WHEN I STIRRED, it was still dark. I checked to the side of me. Grayson and Hunter were still sleeping. Hunter was glued to Grayson's chest.

I took a moment to watch them. They were beautiful together.

I needed a drink of water and to relieve myself. I headed for the kitchen first. We had water drawn from the nearby creek in a ceramic container to keep it somewhat cold.

Thirst quenched, I went outside. I was finished draining my bladder when a set of arms encircled my waist. The height of them told me it wasn't Grayson.

I shivered with delight at the single kiss in the middle of my spine. I closed my eyes and moaned as Hunter's hard cock slipped between my legs. His hands moved to my hips. He rocked forward and back, mating with my thighs, sending tingles to my balls.

My cock lengthened.

Hunter touched my shoulders and turned me around to face him.

In the darkness, I couldn't see him. It was infuriating not having my wolf vision. Our Omega had the most ethereal features. I dreamed of the day I would know him better. Grayson had found something in Hunter that brought on feelings of love. I wouldn't be far behind.

"Couldn't sleep?" I asked him.

"I rolled over and you weren't there."

"I needed some water."

"Was it everything you dreamed it would be … the claiming?"

I laughed. "More. So much more."

"I loved watching it. You two together. The love flowing between you." Hunter wrapped his hand around my hard cock and stroked it. "I'd like to do that again sometime—watch."

There was a broad tree to my right.

The thought of Hunter watching Grayson and me mate again was enough to complete my desire for him. I guided him to the tree. He used his hands to keep the bark from rubbing his chest. He moaned sweetly as I entered him. I placed my hands on his hips and set a steady pace.

"Oh, my god … yes." Hunter lowered his head and pushed his ass against me. His throat opened and he released a continuous string of sounds of pleasure.

Loud.

I didn't care who heard us. Hunter was our Omega. My urge to mate with him was too strong to ignore. I could hear Grayson wander out of the cabin and approach us.

He kissed the back of my neck and ran his finger into my hole. He thrust it as high as he could. The dual sensation had me on the verge of howling. I released a roaring groan instead.

I growled and licked the area on Hunter where Grayson had claimed him. The high was nearly at its peak. I swore at incredible volume as Grayson's cock entered me and I reached the edge of the crest. He pumped into me as I thrust my cock into Hunter. We soon had a rhythm that worked for all three of us. Our bodies moved in time with each other.

I kissed the base of Hunter's neck. Grayson kissed mine. He moved his arms and wrapped them around both of us as best as he could. We were one pumping, writhing mass.

The scent of wolves approaching didn't register at first.

Chapter Eleven | Grayson

I hurriedly slipped my cock from Bryant's hole, turned around, and stretched out my arms to protect my two mates. We'd been so wrapped up in each other that we'd ignored our senses.

"Jeezus." A female Alpha wolf stepped forward. "What the hell is going on out here? We were on patrol, checking the border. We can hear you from the creek."

She had two other male wolves with her. One Omega. One Alpha.

Bryant stepped from behind me. We positioned ourselves so Bryant's sister wouldn't see Hunter. We needed to protect our Omega. I loved him and we might have put a pup in him already.

"This is our private business, Carina," Bryant said.

Carina growled. "It is the business of the pack. Lucas will be told."

"Lucas already knows."

Carina shook her head in confusion and glared at Bryant. "Impossible." She stepped to one side and looked around us. "You have an Omega in there."

She stepped forward and pointed at me. "And you … you were attempting to seed an Alpha."

"We're claimed mates," Bryant said. "All three of us."

Carina recoiled and wrinkled her nose. "That's debauchery."

Bryant snarled and poised himself to shift. "Don't insult my family."

"That's not a family." She sneered. "I knew it was a mistake letting you back in the pack. You're unstable, brother. This proves it. Mating with an Alpha? It's disgusting."

"It's not. We love each other."

"You can't even breed each other." Carina laughed. "Is that why you have the Omega?"

It was my turn to speak. "Even if our Omega had been an Alpha, we would have ended up with him. I love him. He was the piece we needed to complete us."

"That's fucked up," someone in the crowd of wolves said.

Bryant tensed. "Leave us in peace, Carina."

Carina scowled at him. "We'll discuss this tomorrow with Lucas and the pack."

Then the battle of wills started. Who would say *Alpha* first. Bryant stood his ground and kept up a low steady growl as he stared at Carina. His canines descended.

Carina snorted. "Alpha." Then spun on her heel, directed the two wolves to follow her, and disappeared into the trees.

I reached for Bryant's arm. "Your sister is intense."

"Seems to run in the family."

"I guess the pack will know now."

Bryant nodded. "They're already talking. Carina woke everyone."

"Let's go back to bed," Hunter said. "Nothing we can do about it tonight."

We went back into the cabin and arranged ourselves in bed after I stoked the fire a bit. Hunter in the middle. I supported my head in my hand so I could enjoy him. The firelight danced on his smooth skin. His body looked golden in the light. My love for him felt neverending.

Hunter rolled toward me, pushed himself up on his knees, and then straddled my hips. He stroked my soft cock as he leaned down and kissed me. It hardened in his gentle hand.

He straightened and guided my cock to his hole. With a long groan, he sank on my entire length. Seated, he rotated his hips, enjoying the feeling of my cock buried deep inside.

He pulled away enough that I could thrust up into him. Swearing and gasping, he rode my increasingly vigorous battering. He placed his hand on my chest. I took it to mean stop.

"Bryant," Hunter said, reaching out to Bryant. "Join us."

Hunter lay flat on my chest and tipped his ass up.

Bryant moved toward us. He lay a row of kisses down Hunter's entire spine. He ended at his hole. He licked the base of my cock and then the stretched area where we were joined. He sucked and licked and played with the edge of Hunter's hole with his fingers.

I closed my eyes, my heart rate kicking up a notch as Bryant tucked his fingers into Hunter's hole. My cock almost slipped free as he pulled Hunter's hole open.

I wished I could see.

Bryant straddled my thighs. He looked down at me with such love in his eyes. Then his gaze dropped to Hunter. There was something new there. I could see it building.

It made my heart sing.

The pressure was incredible as Bryant fed his cock in alongside mine inside Hunter's hole. The stroke was slow, allowing Hunter time to adjust. I kept my hands on either side of Hunter's face, checking in with him. He kept nodding and licking his lips with the occasional grimace.

Bryant clung to Hunter's chest. Retreated and thrust.

Hunter gasped and tears formed in his eyes.

"Again," he whispered.

Bryant was hesitant but he pulled back and surged forward.

"Yeah," Hunter said. "Yeah … that's it … please."

I buried my heels in the bedding, giving me some leverage. I pushed my cock up into Hunter as Bryant did the same. The sound coming from Hunter nearly made me spill.

Such a seductive groan. A wolf reaching a level of ecstasy that I didn't know was attainable. He clawed my chest, leaving strips of stinging flesh as we pushed into him again.

We alternated our thrusts, our cocks rubbing back and forth against each other, coated in the abundant slickness of Hunter's hole. It was sublime. Pumping into him like pistons.

Our Omega became crazed, panting and looking around wildly.

"Seed me," he pleaded, his voice shaky and low.

"We're going to put a pup in you," I growled.

"Please." Hunter panted harder. "Please."

I grunted as I knotted. Bryant knotted too. Neither of us could bury our knot without hurting Hunter. Instead, our mounds of swollen flesh caressed each other as we squirmed. It was a sensation I'd like to repeat sometime. Just holding our knots together and stroking them.

My climax built, increasing the pressure in my cock. I clawed at Bryant's thighs as my hips lifted, my knot released, and I flooded the inside of our Omega.

After a few clenches of my ass, drilling slowly into Hunter, I slipped from him, allowing Bryant to insert his knot. He was able to continue caressing Hunter's hole until he bucked his hips forward. I felt his copious seed drool onto my balls.

His cock dropped from Hunter's hole, landing on mine.

"On your back," Bryant said to Hunter.

He had to be aching. Hunter complied—but slowly. Bryant encouraged Hunter to hold his legs open, knees up. Then he lay on the bed on his stomach between them.

I came around behind Bryant.

Hunter's hole was swollen, pink, and wet. Wide open. Our white seed decorated the creases. I'd never seen anything more sensual and provocative. Bryant repeatedly sank his finger into the depth of Hunter's hole, collecting and pushing the seed inside him.

My Alpha wanted pups as much as I did.

IT WAS BRIGHT when I woke. Bryant was staring at the ceiling, Hunter curled up against him asleep. Hunter was warming to Bryant. It wouldn't be long until Hunter saw what I did in Bryant. How sweet, caring, and gentle he was. And how loving and protective.

"What are you thinking about?" I asked.

"Just listening to the conversation Carina started with the pack."

After Bryant claimed Hunter and me, we would be eligible to interact with his pack but it would've been too suspicious to ask. There was no reason for the pack to let us in.

It was infuriating.

"And?" I asked.

"Hard to say."

Hunter was lying on Bryant's arm, tucked in against Bryant's neck. Bryant gave him a little squeeze and kissed his head.

"You're glad you became his Alpha," I prompted.

"He's special. I'm drawn to him. He intrigues and excites me. He brings me calm *and* he brings out all sorts of protective emotions. Our lives wouldn't feel complete without him."

I smiled and sought out Bryant's hand to hold. "Well, you know how I feel about him."

He squeezed my hand. "I love that you love him."

"You're not jealous?"

"Why would I be? He brings you joy. Your heart is what I cherish most about you. To see it filled with love makes *my* heart soar with elation. You're my life. You're my love."

"I am so glad I said something to you. That I'm in love with you. What we have now is stunning. I don't care what anyone thinks. I love you and that's never going away. You're my heart."

Hunter coughed and lifted his head. "You two are nauseating."

"I thought you were sleeping," I said.

"All your love chatter woke me."

"How are feeling this morning? Sore?" Bryant asked.

"Feels like someone drove a bus through my ass." Hunter groaned as he sat up and rolled onto one hip. "Other than that … peachy. I may need to avoid sitting, though."

I would have laughed if I hadn't been so distracted. We were all awake now. I needed more information about what Carina was saying and how the pack was reacting. I enjoyed the feeling of belonging to a pack again. I didn't want that to disappear.

I didn't want to go back to the forest. It was too hard to raise pups in the forest.

Impossible even.

You couldn't keep a pup out of wolf form living in the trees without building some sort of home. They needed clothing and fire to keep them warm.

I didn't want to leave here.

I sat up.

"What are they saying?" I asked. "What's the consensus?"

"Lucas is advocating for us." Bryant frowned. "Adam isn't sure. Carina is against letting us continue. Five of the eight wolves are against us. Mama is annoyed but believes it's our choice."

I drew in a long breath and exhaled.

"When do they vote?"

"Any minute now."

Hunter ran his fingers up and down Bryant's chest, brushing his fingers through the abundant black hair. "I'll follow you anywhere. I trust you."

I leaned in and kissed Hunter's shoulder.

He turned his body to face me and cupped my jaw.

"And you." He graced me with a soft and quick kiss on my lips. "I *love* you."

It felt like a molten surge from a volcano. Every emotion I contained erupted at once. It reached my eyes first, tearing them up, and then my lips. I'd never smiled so hard.

Hunter loved me too.

I kissed him and held on tightly as if he might take it back. I wanted to seal his mouth. To keep those words forever between us. Bryant appeared behind Hunter and tucked in close behind him. He nuzzled the back of his ear, his hot breath reaching my cheek.

"You're perfection," he said to Hunter.

I took a chance and released Hunter. He said it again.

"I love you, Grayson."

"I love you too, Omega," I replied.

"We both do," Bryant said.

What?

Bryant *loved* Hunter. I broke out in full sobs. I realized then that whatever the pack decided, it didn't matter. There was so much love between us that we could make anything work.

As long as we're together, we could be anywhere.

"They're voting," Bryant said. "Jonas is abstaining to keep the numbers uneven."

I wrapped my arms around my mates and hung on.

"With my vote," Bryant said, "we have 6 for and 6 against. Adam holds the deciding vote."

I closed my eyes and waited. If Adam hadn't truly forgiven Bryant, we were out of the pack. It was taking far too long. The future of my family might change in an instant.

Bryant let out a long breath and laughed.

"He decided to give us a chance. Adam voted for us to stay."

Hunter leaped around between our bodies. We went from elation to celebration. We both started kissing Hunter. We would be gentle with him, but we were going to mate with him again.

We had a full day and night to mate with each other.

To fill our Omega with seed.

To increase our family.

To create *our* pups.

Chapter Twelve | Hunter

The next 5 weeks flew by. Painting that church to completion. A few odd jobs. Giving my Alphas pointers in running a painting business. Going back to the cabin. Trying to get some sleep after being ravaged by my mates. Then I woke to more glorious intimate time with them.

My life was perfect.

I had moved into the cabin with my Alphas. It was cramped but it was cozy. Although, this past month, I'd been cursing the lack of a proper bathroom in the cabin. Being able to rest my forehead against the cold porcelain of a toilet would have been a relief. Instead, I was forced to find a tree to cling to while I emptied my guts onto the forest floor.

I was pregnant and our pup was growing fast.

I wandered into *Growlers* after giving a quote to a human to paint their front entry. It was a small job but I was losing my desire to be around paint.

It made me feel queasy.

Jonas looked me up and down as I approached the counter.

"Your Alphas work fast," he said, pointing at my swelling belly. It was impossible to hide. The human I quoted probably wouldn't hire me because of it. I was a pregnant male Omega. Humans didn't have much respect for us. I was lucky the human had been so civil.

I placed my hand on my stomach. I had a persistent thought.

"I think it might be twins," I said.

"I think you might be right. Have you spoken to Adam?"

"No." But I knew I should. His last pregnancy had produced twin pups. He would be able to fill me in on what to expect. Exactly how bad was the pain in my back going to get?

It was already brutal.

"Might be a good idea," Jonas said. "The whelping went on a lot longer. Even for someone as productive as Adam, he struggled to maintain his breathing. You might want to practice with him."

Wow. That seemed like a lot. Talking to Adam was one thing. Taking breathing lessons from him was another. I sighed. I had questions about chestfeeding as well.

"Did Adam shift to wolf form when he fed his twins?"

Jonas shook his head. "No, he preferred to suckle them against his bare chest."

I nodded. That was appealing; fur against skin. "I'll go talk to him."

I shifted to wolf form just outside town, hiding my clothes in a wooden box built for that purpose. I shook out my extremely rare all-red fur. Bryant and Grayson had been shocked to see it. I was surprised they hadn't heard of my sire. He was red as well but he tended to keep to himself.

The belief was that all red wolves had been hunted into non-existence back before humans knew some wolves also lived out of wolf form. Partially true. Red wolves like myself and my sire *had* been massacred for their unusual pelts into near extinction but some had survived.

As for my pregnancy.

Before the shift in human awareness, it had been customary to hide pregnant male Omegas away in the forest. Our introduction into human society had been troubled.

Even now, we were shunned.

I ran through the forest, headed for the cabin to redress. I needed to stretch my legs and my back didn't hurt as badly in wolf form. Nothing hurt as badly in wolf form. Even pregnant, my body was muscular and powerful. I could protect my pups if I needed to.

I also needed to stay aware of what was being said in the pack.

After some arguing by Bryant, the pack had let Grayson and me in on the inner dialog of the pack. So far the negative discourse had been minimal. Two of the wolves in the East Creekside pack in particular *did* go out of their way to ridicule us through the pack's link.

They couldn't get past the idea of two Alpha males mating. To them, it didn't make sense. Alpha males couldn't bear pups. Therefore, it was abhorrent.

They didn't understand the love between the three of us. After Bryant told me he loved me, my feelings for him changed. The way he showed his love through kisses and nibbles and sighs of, "My sweet Omega,", and the way he was fierce in protecting me, I had eventually fallen for him. Our love was complete. It went all ways; all three of us were in love with each other.

I shifted outside the cabin and went inside. I was slow to dress. I'm not sure why Adam scared me so much. Maybe because of what Bryant did to him. I was afraid Adam might make me feel uncomfortable or refuse to even welcome me into his home.

I needn't have worried. Adam smiled at me as he opened the door. Then laughed as he caught sight of my belly. His first words to me … "Oh, dear."

"Come in," Adam said and stepped back. I could hear pups growling and yipping in another room. "They're supposed to be napping."

"Something to look forward to."

"As long as they're out of my hair for a few minutes, I don't care if they sleep."

I followed Adam into the kitchen. It was spotless. Not sure how he did it with 8 pups. I had started deep cleaning the cabin. I had no idea how we would manage with twin pups in the space.

"Would you like some ginger tea," Adam asked.

I sighed with relief. "Yes, please. This nausea is getting old."

Adam filled the kettle with water and placed it on the stove. "I found it was worse with the twins." He lifted down two cups. Put a tea bag in one and cut up some ginger for the other.

"I have so many questions," I said.

"Let's start at the beginning. How many weeks do you think you are?"

"Around five, I think."

"Twins?"

"Pretty sure at this point." I pointed at my belly. "Look at me."

"From the first mating most likely."

"Maybe even the rutting before we were mated."

"Do you know whose it might be?"

That was an odd question. Maybe Adam didn't understand our relationship fully. Every night and every morning, they both left me dripping with their seed.

"I'm their Omega. Both of them fill me."

"Okay. I wasn't sure." Adam waved his hand. "Don't mind me. I wasn't sure of the details."

"We love each other. All three of us. We're mated. I'm carrying *our* pups."

Adam studied my face for a moment. "All right. Five weeks. Your back hurting?"

"Killing me."

"Try some willow bark tea. It's safe for the pups. It'll help."

"How big did you get?"

"You're going to get twice that size. The pups might come early. Just not enough room in there for both of them. Mine didn't, though. I couldn't get out of bed for the final two weeks."

"That sounds miserable."

Adam winked at me. "My Alpha kept me entertained."

That was another question I had. "Can we keep mating?"

"Absolutely. Positioning gets difficult. I was riding Lucas with our first pup when my water broke. If you go past 8 weeks, I would recommend lots of mating. It stimulates whelping."

"And what's that like … whelping?"

"Painful. But don't be scared. It's natural and totally worth it."

I furrowed my brow. I *was* scared. Having to whelp two pups instead of one meant I'd need to push twice. It was twice the pain. I took the cup Adam offered me. And twice the reward.

"Jonas suggested you coach me on breathing."

"Sure. I can do that. We can meet once a week. Late evening works best when the pups are in bed." He took a sip of his tea and then set it down. "You'll be fine. You're a strong wolf."

I appreciated that. I was average for an Omega in height but in addition to knitting and painting, I spent a lot of my free time running through the forest and hunting.

I was healthy and I was muscular for an Omega.

"You chose to chest feed out of wolf form. Why?"

Adam sighed. "Mostly because I like holding them in my arms as they feed. Looking down into their little faces. Playing with their paws. Tickling their tummies to keep them awake so they keep feeding until they're full. You can't do any of those things in wolf form."

"I like that. We'll see after they're whelped how I feel."

Adam shifted gears. "I'm glad the three of you found each other."

"It seemed destined. None of us were looking for it."

Adam leaned on the counter, his chin on his hand. "Who did you fall in love with first?"

I smiled. "Grayson. There was an instant connection with us. Even on that first night of rutting with both of them, I knew I wanted to be with him. He's so kind, caring, and loving."

"And Bryant?"

"I wasn't too sure about him at first."

Adam laughed. "Understandable. I don't know him at all really but I've heard stories."

I folded my hands around the warm cup. "His love for Grayson is beautiful. And over the last few weeks, knowing I'm pregnant, he's been incredibly attentive."

"He loved you before you loved him."

"Yes." I laughed. "But I soon succumbed to his charm."

"I can't imagine being loved that fiercely by two Alphas. I have enough trouble managing one. He's like having a ninth pup around sometimes. But he also makes me feel safe and protected."

"He views you as an equal."

"Always has. We work well as the fated mates leading this pack." Adam tapped his cup. "How does that work with the three of you? Have you hunted together yet?"

I stood up straight. "Every week. Our link works well. We hunt efficiently through it."

"If you need any additional meat just ask Jonas. The bison is best."

"I'll keep that in mind." I finished my tea. "I really should have a nap before my Alphas get home. It was great to be able to ask you all these questions. I'm sure I'll have more."

"Come by anytime. I'm almost always here other than teaching my weekly art classes."

"I've always wanted to try that. Paint an actual picture. I'm good with my brushes."

"We have a painting class starting in a week. You should join."

"I'll think about it." I followed Adam to the door. "Thank you again. I was a little worried about coming here. I've never spoken to you before … and everything else."

"That's behind us. You're part of the pack now. So is Bryant. And Grayson. It'll take a while but soon everyone will move on to something else to complain about."

I waved goodbye and headed down the steps. It had been nice of Adam to invite me to the painting classes. I'd have to give it a miss this time. Even the thought of paint made me feel queasy.

I might have to go on something the humans called maternity leave.

I was shivering by the time I reached the cabin.

Winter had hit last week. No snow but it was chilly. I looked at the cold dead fireplace and considered starting a fire. Decided I was too tired. I stripped, shifted to wolf form, and curled up on the area rug in front of the hearth. When I woke, the fire was roaring.

I could hear my Alphas in the kitchen, talking and laughing quietly so as not to wake me.

Hunter: *"You do have inner voices, you know."*

Bryant: *"Sorry. Talking is a nice change after all of those years in our heads."*

"I prefer speaking aloud," Grayson said.

I stretched, doing my best downward dog, and then shifted.

"How are you feeling today, Omega?" Bryant asked.

"Nauseous and sore." I padded into the kitchen and poured myself a glass of water. "I went to see Adam today. To ask him a few questions."

"How did that go?" asked Grayson.

"He had lots of good information … because I'm pretty sure I have news for you both."

Bryant placed his hand on my stomach. "Everything all right in there?"

"Perfect," I answered, "for both of them."

Grayson's eyes opened wide and Bryant released a short laugh.

"Twins?" In stereo.

It brought tears to my eyes to see how excited they were. There was only one thing missing. My sire should know about my incredible life. He'd always been supportive of me. He had invested in my painting business when my pack leader turned me away.

I wasn't sure how he'd feel about this.

"What's wrong?" Grayson asked. My tears had turned from joy to sorrow. They had both detected the change. They crowded around me and held me.

"I want to tell my sire. Tell him about the twins. Introduce you both."

Bryant held me at arm's length. "How will he react?"

I shrugged. "Hard to say. He stays away from pack life. Doesn't agree with the politics. I don't know if the structure of wolf mating relationships plays into that."

"Is he in Riverton?" Grayson asked.

"Okay ... see, that's the thing. He could be anywhere due east of there."

"How far east?"

"I'm told two days on paw."

"That'll put you well into your second semester," Bryant said.

"It'll be impossible to travel with pups," I replied. "I don't think we can go any other time."

"I don't like this," Grayson said.

"Please, Grayson. I'll be fine."

"Only if we leave early tomorrow morning," Bryant said. "There's no snow in the forecast for the next week." He moved around the cabin in thought. "We'll make better time on ATVs."

"And frighten him off," I replied. "He'll be long gone before we find him."

"ATV for 8 hours in and then we shift," Grayson said.

I could concede to that. We would be far enough from him that he wouldn't hear the engines. Another day or more in furs and we would be close to him. I could howl to alert him to visitors.

Hopefully, he'd respond.

"I need to arrange to borrow an extra machine," Bryant said. "Lucas only has two."

It sounded like we had a plan. In two days, I'd see my sire for the first time in 7 years. Last I'd seen him, I'd been 15 and not able to shift to wolf form yet. I had come to him to ask his help to start my painting business. He'd left pack life two days after that. A lot had changed.

I looked back and forth between my two Alphas and touched my stomach.

I was in love and expecting pups.

Maybe that would be enough.

Chapter Thirteen | Bryant

We had my truck, Lucas', and Jonas' all loaded with one ATV each and plastic containers of gasoline to strap to the machines once we unloaded them. Hunter had checked with the pack leader in Riverton. We had permission to use them on the Riverton pack's territory.

In addition to the gasoline, we loaded up with extra clothes in case the temperature dropped while we were en route on the ATVs. I felt uneasy as we took off.

Once we were in Riverton, we followed a logging road into the forest on the east side of town. Every minute we traveled in that direction was a minute further from home.

We unloaded everything and then Lucas, Adam, and Jonas slipped back into the trucks. All three of them thought we were insane. That Hunter would be too uncomfortable. Our Omega had filled a large plastic bag with willow bark to chew on to keep his back in check.

I didn't like the idea either but Grayson and I would do anything for Hunter. He wanted to see his sire before whelping our pups. I was determined to see that it happened.

We were going to take it easy. There were only animal paths through the forest. Grayson had strapped a chainsaw to his ATV in case we encountered any downed trees.

There were lots of them.

It was slow going.

We were headed for a power right away Hunter insisted was there. His sense of direction was good. He'd been up that way with his friends. We soon uncovered it.

Without the clearing beneath the power lines, it would have been quicker to make the trek as wolves. We picked up speed on the open ground.

After 5 hours, the line started to veer north.

Grayson slowed and stopped. "I don't want to take these things into the bush again." He shut off his engine. "I think we should shift now. It'll be dark in two hours. We can curl up for the night to give Hunter a rest. Start at first light."

"I would love to shift," Hunter said. "Not sure I can chew enough of this painkiller. I need to be in wolf form to give myself and my back a little relief."

"We can turn back if you're in too much pain," I said.

"Absolutely not," Hunter replied and climbed off his machine. He stripped out of his clothes. I smiled. His belly was round and firm and his nipples had started to swell.

His beautiful red coat emerged as he shifted. I loved everything about Hunter. His ripe full belly, his intelligence, his exquisite face, his cheeky attitude.

And his love for Grayson.

It was pure and good.

Grayson deserved that kind of love.

I shifted and joined Grayson and Hunter at the edge of the forest. Due east was easier to find in wolf form. One became hyperaware of the movement of the sun.

We trotted off, letting Hunter lead the way. We would let him set the pace. Rest when he wanted to rest. His well-being was of utmost importance to both of us.

We made decent time. Kept up a steady pace for what felt like 3 hours. The sun had long set. There wouldn't be much chatter as we settled in and curled up against each other. Inner dialog was difficult in wolf form. Like a block was thrown up stopping intelligent conversation.

We needed to shift out of wolf form to do that; speak.

It was too cold to be without furs.

I snuggled in and fell asleep.

When we awoke the next morning, there was a light dusting of snow covering us. We rose and shook it off. Grayson whined and Hunter comforted him, nudging his muzzle.

Our Omega was determined to continue.

We traveled an entire day without encountering any signs that a wolf was traveling and hunting the area. We spent a second night beneath the boughs of a cedar tree.

Hunter was anxious to start the next morning. Snow was falling steadily now. We embarked on day three. We stopped every two hours to rest. Not for long. Just enough time for Hunter to recover sufficiently to continue. Close to nightfall, Hunter jogged to a slow stop.

I inhaled. It was faint but I detected a wolf. Older. Alpha.

I wandered up beside Hunter and nudged him with my shoulder.

He sneezed and nodded his head.

Hunter sat back on his haunches and let sound build in his chest. Clear and loud, he howled a message of presence. That we were here. That Hunter was of his pack.

Hunter's tone changed when a wolf in the distance joined him. Hunter sang a song about family. Of the wolf being his sire. The song was answered. We'd found the right wolf.

Hunter looked at me and blinked. Something was bothering him. It was bothering me too. The wolf's song had been weak. Grayson joined us and whined. He sensed it too.

We headed toward where we had heard the wolf. After an hour, a small shack appeared through the trees. There was no smoke rising from the small chimney.

The stench coming from the structure was overpowering.

Hunter was the first to approach. Only a piece of oil cloth protected the indoors from the outdoors. Hunter pushed the material aside with his muzzle and went inside.

He emerged nearly a minute later—shifted.

"He needs help," Hunter said.

Grayson and I shifted. Walking through the snow barefoot was uncomfortable. The cold wind bit my skin. Hunter headed back inside and we followed.

Our senses were assaulted as we entered the shack. The smell was rotting flesh. And it was coming from a red wolf lying on his right side, panting on a makeshift bed.

Hunter's sire.

"His leg is infected," Hunter said.

"I'm going to start a fire." Grayson got to work arranging some kindling and wood in a small fireplace. "We should start by cleaning that wound."

I squatted near the bed structure and moved some fur aside to get a better look. His back left hock was mangled. Not only was it infected, but his tibia appeared to be broken.

It had to have been a boar. Taking one down as a lone wolf was never a good idea. They fought back and they were vicious with tusk-like teeth that could rip you apart.

That had to be what happened to Hunter's sire.

"I smell a creek nearby," I said to Hunter. I looked around. "Use that container over there and collect some water." Grayson had flames started. It brought some much needed light.

"I can do it," Grayson said. "Omega … put on some clothes. It's freezing in here." He took the container with him as he left the shack. I could start debriding the wound.

"Find a knife," I said to Hunter once he was dressed in some clothes that were far too big for him. His sire was a large wolf. "I need to cut some of this dead flesh away."

I placed my hand on the sire's thigh. "It would be better if you shifted …." I looked at Hunter. "What's his name?"

"Bracken."

I looked back at the wolf. His eyes were closed. He was breathing heavily. Howling a response had taken a lot out of him. "Bracken, I need you to shift. I can't work through all this fur."

Bracken groaned but his bones began to change. The shift was slow and arduous. He cried and whined through each major change. His injured leg was the last to shift.

It looked worse like this. Without the fur, I could see the extent of the damage. It was obvious it had been a boar. I took the knife Hunter handed me. This was going to hurt.

I heated the knife in the fire to sanitize it and let it cool.

"Cover him up with a fur," I said to Hunter. "Keep him still."

"Just about to." Hunter pulled a bear fur off a rack and placed it over Bracken. I kneeled and picked at the edge of the wound, lifting dead pieces of flesh. Bracken screamed as I sliced away the first area of necrotic tissue. Hunter held him down by lying on Bracken's side.

I worked as quickly as I could. Grayson arrived with the water just in time to help clear the blood away so I could see what I was doing. Grayson handed me a cloth. It wasn't as clean as I would have liked, but it's all I had. I rubbed water on the wound until I was satisfied.

"Hunter, do you know how to make a poultice for this?"

"Not sure I can find everything in the snow."

"I'll go with you," Grayson said as he lifted down some clothes for himself. It must be getting colder. The fire was barely heating the space.

"I'm going to try to reset the bone." There were long sticks near the fire used for poking at the logs. They'd make a good splint. I'd need to tear up a shirt to bind the sticks. That would leave nothing for me to wear if we were going to cart Bracken out of here. He needed proper medical attention. Hunter would have to shift back to wolf form so I could have his clothes.

My two mates left the shack. I retrieved the sticks and a shirt and began tearing it into strips. The next part would be more difficult. I needed to line the bones up properly. It would relieve some of the pain and any healing that started to happen would be correctly positioned.

Again, the screaming. And no one to hold Bracken down. He reached for me and fought with my hands. It was a difficult struggle but I finally had his leg splinted.

Bracken gasped and cried. He was exhausted. He must have been like this for days. No way to call anyone. It had been absolute providence and luck that had brought us to him.

Hunter ducked into the shelter with a handful of plant and lichen material. The fungi component would be missing. Wrong season. I prepared a square of cloth from the shirt I had torn up as Hunter put everything he and Grayson had collected into his mouth and started to chew. A mortar and pestle would have been ideal but we needed to improvise.

Grayson came in with more wood for the fireplace. "He has a woodshed."

I thought it odd that Bracken would spend enough time out of wolf form that he needed a shelter as equipped as this one. I looked around. Along one wall were mountains of notebooks.

"Does your sire write?" I asked Hunter.

"Poems. He's obsessed with them."

That would explain it. He needed to be out of wolf form to write.

"We're going to need to stay here for a couple of days before we can move him." I mounded the chewed plant material on the square of cloth and placed it over the wound. It would increase healing and stop the flesh from rotting away again.

"Two of us will have to sleep outdoors at a time," Grayson said. "There's not enough room in here for all of us." He touched Hunter's face. "You stay in here with your sire and the fire."

Hunter grumbled but didn't object. He was as keen to protect our pups as we were. Sleeping outside in the snow would put too much stress on his body.

"We'll leave you to sleep," I said. "Don't let him fuss with the poultice."

Grayson was the first to kiss Hunter. It was a kiss full of emotion. He loved Hunter and he was concerned for him. I showed my affection next, immersing myself in Hunter's love for me.

Grayson stripped, hung up the clothes, and we left the shack. We spent a moment outside in each other's arms. I'd missed his lips. Missed his touch. The cold was the only thing stopping us from mating. Neither of us was compelled to mate in wolf form. It wouldn't be the same.

I needed his arms around me. Holding me. I needed to look into his eyes as my cock thrust into him. I needed his lips on mine as I filled him with my seed.

We reluctantly released each other and shifted. I nudged his muzzle with mine and rubbed shoulders with him, nearly knocking him off balance. We found a bare spot beneath a spruce tree and curled up together. The snowfall was getting worse. I was worried as I fell asleep.

IT WAS THREE DAYS LATER when we agreed that Bracken was well enough to travel. Grayson, Bracken, and I would dress in the sparse offering of winter clothes and support Bracken as we trekked out on snowshoes. Hunter would retain his wolf form to stay warm.

It hadn't stopped snowing. The white blanket was up to our knees. It was going to take us at least a week to get back to the ATVs. Bracken had argued that we should leave him to die. Hunter wasn't hearing it. His sire was the same age as Grayson. Plenty of life left in him.

When Bracken was lucid enough to speak and understand, Hunter had told him about us. That we were three mates. That Grayson and I were both Alphas. That we were expecting pups.

Bracken had scowled at the three of us, a prejudice emerging. He'd gone as far as calling us deviants. But he needed us. Sometime during day two, he softened to us and apologized.

Now we needed to get him out of the forest to a hospital.

We carefully packaged up enough matches to do us. We'd need to stop well before nightfall each day, build a shelter, and start a fire. Also, we needed to continue keeping Bracken and Hunter well fed. Game was scarce. They were existing on a diet of rabbits.

Grayson and I refused to eat. The daily ration of melted snow was all we needed.

On day four, Hunter started to slow down. It was difficult for him to get through the snow even though he followed in the depressions our snowshoes made.

The last few hours, he kept lagging; stopping.

I released Bracken to Grayson and walked back to him.

Bryant: *"What's going on?"*

Hunter: *"Tired. Sore."*

Bryant: *"Your back is bothering you?"*

Hunter: *"Belly."*

Hunter grimaced and began panting. He whined and looked up at me.

Hunter: *"Help."*

"We need to stop," I shouted to Grayson. "Something's wrong with Hunter."

Grayson dumped Bracken in the snow and ran back to us. He slid the last foot on his knees, dislodging his snowshoes, to be at Hunter's eye level. He ran his hand across the top of Hunter's head. He held Hunter's face in both hands and put his forehead on Hunter's.

Grayson: *"What's going on?"*

Hunter: *"Pups. Coming."*

I inhaled sharply.

Bryant: *"Now?"*

Hunter: *"Now."*

I looked at Grayson. "What do we do?"

"He needs somewhere to whelp the pups."

We were in the middle of the bloody forest. I inhaled. There had to be one around somewhere. A large den of any kind would do. I caught the light scent of a badger.

I moved toward it and started scooping snow away from the area around the source. I uncovered it. The den was abandoned.

Bryant: *"Grayson. Help me with this."*

I stripped off my clothes and shifted. Grayson was shifted by my side helping as I started digging through the soil to increase the size of the den. This was the best we could do.

Hunter rubbed against me. He whined as he looked at what we had created for him. This was not the way we had planned on having our pups. We had talked about getting home and curling up in our cozy bed to wait for the pups' arrival. Whelping them in our bed, with Hunter in our arms.

Smothered in kisses and support.

Cuddling together as he suckled the pups for the first time.

Instead, he would be alone down there. He brushed up against Grayson and followed the entrance into the den. Protected from the elements, he curled up to wait.

We needed to build a shelter for Bracken. I regretted not splinting him in wolf form. He would be more difficult to carry out but he'd be able to stay warm without shelter and a fire.

Hunter whining louder caught my attention. I poked my head down into the den. Hunter was panting harder now and squirming around in the small space.

Grayson: *"Hunter?"*

Bryant: *"Soon."*

The one-word sentences were irritating me. I shifted back out of wolf form and redressed. We needed to start cutting some evergreen boughs to make a shelter. Grayson joined me.

By the time we had the shelter and fire built, and Bracken settled, Hunter was breathing hard and lifting his head to sniff near his birthing area. He must be close.

Only one of us could look inside the den at a time. We took turns reaching in and stroking Hunter's fur to comfort him. The contractions started joined by a whimpering whine.

Grayson was on his belly and almost pushed his shoulders into the entrance of the den. I sat behind him. Grayson had fallen in love with Hunter first. It felt right for him to be there with him.

A few minutes later, Grayson pulled out of the den. His hands were covered in slime and blood. The first pup had arrived.

"Is the pup all right?" I asked.

"Small but strong. Hunter cleaned it off. Licked it until it started breathing." He smiled at me. "It has black fur like you."

Hunter: *"Bryant."*

My Omega was calling for me. Grayson shimmied out of the way so I could take up the position he had been in. There was just enough light that I could see. A black pup was tucked up against Hunter's chest, buried in his fur, whimpering and squirming.

Hunter pushed and struggled to reach his birthing area. One final push and a little bundle emerged. A tight little package wrapped in a cocoon. I used my fingers to peel away the coating and expose the pup. I handed it up to Hunter's face. He went to work and stimulated the pup to breathe. It was a glorious sound. I stroked the pup's wet fur. Grey and white like Grayson.

I was in heaven as Hunter continued licking our pups until their fur started to look furry. Hunter lowered his head and closed his eyes. I moved each one and helped them find a nipple.

I backed out of the den.

"They're suckling," I said and grinned. I held Grayson's face and kissed him. "The second one has your coloring. I think they're both of ours."

Grayson's eyes told me everything as tears formed in the corners. He'd been praying for that ever since Hunter had told us we were having twins.

He crawled toward the den and peered in. Just enough that he could see them. He kneeled and then jumped to his feet, and stripped off his clothes. And shifted. The wind was picking up. More snow. He curled up at the entrance to the den, sealing it from the incoming storm.

My mate was fierce in his desire to protect our precious Omega and pups.

To protect our family.

I couldn't have loved him or Hunter more.

They were the loves of my life.

My forever loves.

Chapter Fourteen | Grayson

I awoke a few times to check my surroundings. Each time, I had to peer through a layer of snow covering me. I could hear our pups whimpering behind me. They were awake and feeding again.

The first time they had fallen asleep, I had reached out to Hunter to make sure they were all right. Pups couldn't regulate their temperature for the first week. They had to stay warm.

I was terrified something was going to go wrong.

Bryant plowed through the snow toward me. We had agreed to switch off the next time I stirred. I was looking forward to some time lying in front of the fire.

After I rose, I turned around and stuck my head in the den. Warmth radiated from it. Even though they were early, the pups looked vigorous and healthy. I would feel better once we had them at home in the cabin where the weather wasn't trying to take them from us.

Bryant plopped himself down near the entrance. I moved away so he could check on them. Settle his mind that everything was all right. He curled up in the spot I had created.

Feeling satisfied with his position, I made my way to the shelter. Bracken was asleep, piled high to keep warm with clothes we weren't wearing. The fire needed to be tended to. I shifted out of wolf form to take care of it but quickly shifted back afterward. The gently falling snow of a day ago had turned into a near blizzard. The cold was almost biting through my fur.

I lay down close to the fire. I was nodding off when I heard a buzzing sound. My wolf brain didn't register what it was. Reluctantly, I made yet another shift to gain some clarity.

Snowmachines.

They were a distance off. I howled, knowing the wind would probably carry my sound away from where I wanted it to go. I heard a howl back.

Wolves.

Bryant joined me in howling our reply. We were in trouble. We needed help.

Bryant*: "Lucas."*

I didn't recognize the howl. Bryant did. It was joined by another. And another. Bryant didn't identify them. Hunter did.

Hunter*: "Mark."*

The leader of the Riverton pack.

They came within range and I reached out to Lucas.

Grayson*: "Fire."*

Lucas*: "I can smell it. We'll be right there. Is everyone all right?"*

Grayson*: "We're all safe."*

The sound came closer and then through the snow, I saw them. Five snowmachines. I could make out Lucas' form out front. And another large Alpha I assumed was Mark.

As they drove closer, I could see Adam and two others I didn't recognize. I strode toward them to speak to them as they dismounted.

Lucas jogged through the snow toward me and actually hugged me.

"We're so glad we found you," he said. "When you didn't come back and Mark reported it was snowing out this way, we started to panic."

He looked around. "Where's Bryant?"

I grinned. "Guarding Hunter and the pups."

"Pups!" Lucas pounded me on both shoulders. "Adam told me it might be twins."

"They're early." Adam moved in to hug me as well. "Are they both healthy?"

"Small but robust. Hunter is taking good care of them."

Adam scowled as he perused the area near the fire. "Where is he?"

I pointed toward the den. "Below ground. He whelped in wolf form."

Lucas' eyebrows raised. "That's unusual. He's lucky they were small."

"We were prepared to pull him out of there if he started to have trouble," I replied. That would have been a nightmare, trying to keep Hunter and the pups warm above ground.

"How do we get everyone out of here?" Mark approached our group.

"Did you bring extra clothes?" I asked.

"Figured you might not have any," Lucas said. "Found a couple of heavy coats and a full snowsuit that'll fit Hunter." He pointed toward the den. "He'll be able to tuck the pups inside against his skin. We've got a bear fur as well. We can wrap Hunter in it."

Adam patted my shoulder. "Your pups will be fine."

Mark jerked his chin toward the shelter. "Is that Bracken?"

"Yeah." I nodded. "A boar got him. Found him nearly dead."

Mark laughed and shook his head. "He's a stubborn old wolf living out here on his own." He clapped his hands together. "Okay, so there's four of you. Five of us." He looked at me. "Do you want to drive the snowmachine with your Omega and pups?"

I nodded. "I'd prefer that, yes."

"Bryant can come with me," Lucas said.

"I'll take Bracken," Mark added.

"Then I guess I'll go with one of these sexy wolves you have with you," Adam said.

Lucas growled and Adam laughed. "Calm down, Alpha." He drew Lucas to him and kissed him and then placed his hand on his stomach. "Our love has filled my belly again. I'm yours."

Lucas must have known of the pup already because he simply cupped Adam's face and whispered, "I love you, Omega," before kissing him.

Mark cleared his throat. "Light is fading. We need to go."

Hunter was hesitant to leave the den. His wolf instincts were ruling him. It took a lot of coaxing from Bryant, Adam, and me to get Hunter to let us remove the pups to allow him out.

He shook out his fur and then shifted. He was immediately over at our pups, fussing with them, touching them, and burying his nose in their fur.

"Hunter, put this on." Adam handed him the snowsuit. He needed to be quick to put it on. Even holding them inside our coats, the pups were getting cold. They'd deteriorate fast.

I mounted a snow machine. Hunter tucked the pups against his chest after putting on the snowsuit and wrapped the bear fur around his body. He did his best to hang on as we all set out.

We kept going through the night. Stopping only to fill the gas tanks and let Hunter check on and feed the pups. They were cozy and warm against his skin.

We arrived outside the Riverton pack's housing area after 9 hours of traveling. Lucas and Bryant's trucks were parked in the driveway. The entire area had been hit by snow.

On the road back to Creekside, I felt like I could relax a little. I was exhausted. My arms hurt from steering the snowmachine. Hunter must be close to fainting. The three of us were cuddled up against each other in the cab of Bryant's truck. He had the heat cranked.

I was able to hold the pups and kiss their little furry heads for the first time.

They smelled amazing.

They signified our love for each other.

A unique love that would withstand whatever prejudice was thrown at us.

A love that was pure and good.

A love that would forever keep my heart beating.

Chapter Fifteen | Hunter

It was almost too warm. The fire was roaring. The comforters beneath us on the bed. Bryant was at my back, his arm draped across me. His leg hanging over my thigh. Grayson was facing me, holding my hand, gazing at me. Our pups were taking turns feeding happily.

We arrived home safely a week ago. We had barely separated from each other. Lucas and Jonas had been bringing us meat. Most hours of the day found us sleeping.

My sire had come to visit us. Mark helped him navigate on crutches through the trees from Lucas' house to the cabin. The ordeal had brought our two packs closer together.

And my sire seemed pleased. He'd brought me some new yarn and needles. I'd already started knitting our pups little colorful sweaters. They were both male. Both Alphas.

I was positive each was sired by a different Alpha.

My Alphas.

I repositioned the grey and white pup. We hadn't named them yet. So far the grey one was quiet and the black one seemed demanding and grumpy. Just like their sires.

"I love you," Grayson said and stroked my face.

"I love you too," Bryant said against the back of my neck.

I breathed it in. The love surrounding us. The little black pup whimpered and pawed at the air. Grayson pulled him to his chest, held him in his palm, and kissed his head.

And started humming.

It was a song of happiness and family. Grayson has sung me the words once. Bryant snuggled closer to me. My heart felt close to bursting with joy.

When these two wolves had piled out of that truck to buy my van, I knew we were destined for something. Never had I thought my life would become so full with them.

I closed my eyes.

This moment was a gift.

A gift as beautiful as our life together was.

Did you love this story? Do you want to read about Mark and his love story?

Look for *Mark's Chosen* by JT Fader
An MM Wolf Shifter MPreg Romance

About the Author

JT Fader is an alternate pen name for Leigh Jarrett (she/he), allowing Leigh to explore their love of MM+ paranormal and fantasy stories by creating their own worlds.

In their hometown of Victoria, BC, Canada, Leigh can be found nestled up with their fabulously supportive wife and trusty laptop or enjoying the wondrous Vancouver Island outdoors.

To stay up to date with JT Fader's new releases and promos, check out their JT Fader Fantasticals website at www.jtfader.com.

You can also find Leigh on Bluesky.